JOIN my
LEON M
A EDWARDS
CLUB

Leon M A Edwards Club members get free books, ahead of publications. So you can enjoy the book and form an opinion of how it made you feel.

Members only get emails about any promotions and when the next book is ready to receive.

See the back of the book for details on how to sign up.

Six Weeks

Friends To Lovers Romance Novel

Leon M A Edwards

Thriller and Intense Limited

Subscribers only get emails about future new e-book releases to receive for free. We do not send marketing material.

See also back of the book for details on how to sign up.

SUBSCRIBE

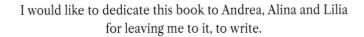

I would like to dedicate this book to Andrea, Alina and Lilia
for leaving me to it, to write.

Acknowledgments

♥

Thank God for giving me the confidence to start writing and the ability to write a story.

Contents

Him

Week 1

It is the beginning of July and I have a sense this year will be an excellent year for me. I recently acquired a new client in Los Angeles who has a business which is a going concern. The owner has a media company which is struggling to stay afloat and compete in the magazine market. It requires traveling from New York, where my business is based, to be hands on with my coworkers to assess the company. To see where we can save money and people's livelihood.

I expect it will take a month to salvage the company. Then nurture the business remotely in New York until I feel it can standalone without support.

My name is Richard Lewis and I own a consulting firm analyzing company statement of income, financial position and cash flow. Even though it sounds difficult, it is quite simple to assess the performance of a company and find a solution to the problem. I established my consultancy business twenty years ago.

I am a black African American in my late thirties and five foot six. I shave my hair completely off and keep a clean-shaven face. My skin is dark brown and my chest has slight hairs.

My body is slim and athletic through cardio exercise, such as going on the treadmill and cycling machine. I never found an interest in weights.

Work colleagues would say I am reserved with a dry sense of humor and able to articulate my thoughts and read people. I believe it has come from devoting time to observing people's behaviors and seeing a pattern in similar like-minded people.

When I finished my studies in Business and Accounting, I worked for an accountancy firm for five years before working for myself. I spent fifteen years building up a portfolio of over two hundred clients, providing ongoing advice and preparing business plans for future funding.

I have been single all my life and devoted my time to building my business and creating a great team around me.

The only clothes I wear are tailor made three-piece suits I buy every six months out of boredom. My wardrobe is full of twenty suits and equally tailor fitted corporate shirts with double cufflink. I like the comfort of wearing silky smooth suits as opposed to social, casual wear.

I go to Los Angeles at the weekend and begin work on Monday. I have had my secretary organize flights and accommodation for my staff to live and work while we are there.

My team of five financial experts are accompanying me to save a company from liquidation and revolutionize their dated internal printing machines.

It is Friday late afternoon, around four o'clock. There is a cup of coffee in my hand. I have my tie loose and my shirt sleeves pulled up after a long day. I allow my staff to finish work early today so I am alone in my building except for my secretary who insists on ensuring staying on.

My secretary is not the typical woman you would hear in an erotic love novel. She is not a blonde six foot two long legged sexy woman. Instead, she is a quaint older lady in her seventies with young grandchildren. She sees me like a son. Her name is Valerie, and she reminds me of a version of Miss Marple. She is Caucasian with a pale complexion but aged well.

Valarie comes into my office to confirm my itinerary. 'Your flight is Sunday at two o'clock. I have booked you into a rental house with a single floor and pool. It is quiet and quaint. You will do your work in peace.'

I continue to stare out of the window down at the street below until she finishes talking. 'Thank you Valarie. Take the month off and spend time with your family. You can't do anything here while I'm gone.'

Valerie gives me a sad look, like I am a stray dog. 'I think you have worked hard enough to make this business the best you can. It is time to meet someone. Let your people take the reins. You're successful now.'

I smile with embarrassment. 'Its finding someone who will have me. That is the problem. If you were ten years younger, I would ask you to come for a coffee. I don't know. Ask you to the cinema and see where it leads.'

Valarie blushes at me. 'If I were ten years younger, I would marry you. You should be happy. You're a good man. There is more to life than work.'

I hear her but it is easier than done. 'I am difficult to get along with. When women rearrange your house, mix their toothbrush with yours. I don't like that. Wear my shirts in the morning. And all that intimacy. My life is what it is and I like it. I know where I'm going next. I am not climbing the walls wondering if she will have me.'

Valarie gives me a gentle smile. 'You should have a safe trip and see you when you return.'

I watch her walk away round the corner with her handbag clutched to her waist and think of her as my grandma.

After I leave the office, I walk through the financial district pedestrian area and cross over Water Street to head to a small restaurant for dinner, before I head home to my house outside New York. I take in the busy noise of taxi cabs honking and sound of foot traffic along the sidewalk. Walking allows me time to consider up-and-coming work and occasionally reflect on my single life. I wonder if a certain person exists for me or comes to terms. I will not experience the warmth of a woman or love.

It is not long now before I reach my destination.

I choose to sit by the window so I can people watch while having a lovely meal with excellent wine. I observe strangers through the restaurant window and guess whether they are single or with someone. Assume if they are going home to an empty house or a family. I wonder if they have a similar lifestyle to me with the big house and fancy car in the drive or have the simple life of a family car and a reasonably priced home.

My mind wonders to a girl I once knew in college and wonders if it would have gone anywhere. I had a lot of reservations about her. She was outgoing, and I liked my space. She was loud, and I was quiet. I found she had annoying habits, like always asking if I am okay or taking my fries before eating them. She wanted to know everything I was doing. But she had a cute nose and a nice bum. Her eyes were dark brown and lovely to stare into them. But, my mind was on my studies and nothing else. I kept finding faults to stop myself from detracting from my dream of becoming a successful financial person. I wonder what she is doing right now.

When I get home after six o'clock, I stoke the fireplace and open a bottle of wine and sit in my armchair and watch the flames light up the room. I set my house up like a family home as I like to feel relax and have a proper home. I have never brought a woman home. It is silent, with no traffic noise or neighbors. I listen to smooth music such as Sade 'smooth operator' to help me drift into my space and not think about work. I love watching films on the weekend. A cross between an action romance film to a soppy movie where boy meets girl. It reminds me of what kind of relationship I may want in the future.

I live in New Jersey in the suburbs near woodlands. From the outside, my house appears run down with slatted wood on the outside is drab and almost weathered. There is a quaint little porch with steps leading up to it. I have a small patch of grass outside with flower beds, but no flowers. I drive a car but only use it locally, as driving into New York is not fun.

Inside, I renovated the floor boards with fresh solid flooring and stained in a light brown colored paint with a varnish effect. I chose neutral colors in my home such as cream, white and beige colors in all the rooms to lighten up the place. Outside, can be a little gloomy during the winter period and so I wanted my house to be light and warm. My sofas are fabric and beige, with turquoise cushions and a plain glass coffee table.

I bought the house at a steal as it was properly run down and my secretary thought I was mad. But I visualized how it could look. I cleared the garden of garbage, using a man and his van, and then landscaped it flat with two levels and shrubs along the perimeter. I had a stone patio area laid and a fresh lawn.My house has five double bedrooms, each with two rooms having an ensuite. I had the bathrooms installed and revamped the downstairs toilet. I made it like a family home in case I moved and wanted it to sell with ease.

The fire place is cream with a mix of faint vein like black lines with a marble effect.

Saturday morning, I go for a light jog around the local estate for half an hour, then shower and pack a month's worth of suits and shirts. I decide to take six suits and two weeks' worth of work shirts to go with my suits. I can choose what I wear daily. After I finish packing, I knock on my neighbor's door to ask her to overlook my house while away on business.

My neighbor is a young woman with a high-flying job being an interior decorator. She had a similar idea with the doer upper. I more or less copied her home decor when I first came to her house. She has not been to my house and so she does not know the interior of my house is a replacer of her place. She was one of the first neighbors to welcome me before renovating the property.

Her name is Rachael, and she is in her late twenties with wealthy parents and so able to be eccentric in her choice of career. She is tall, brunette with shapely legs with an olive skin. I notice her natural beauty and believe she would not have an interest in me. She is a free spirit and confident while I like structure and have average features. I know she would hurt me and not recover from her.

She opens the door in a bath towel and ignores me at the door. I thought she would check her window before allowing me to see her with wet skin and her towel barely covering her bum. I focus on her shoulders as she turns her back on me.

I make it brief why I knocked. 'I am not staying for long, broaching your privacy.'

Rachael waves her hand at me. 'Don't worry. I'm going out with my girlfriends. Thought it would be easier to talk while I am finishing drying myself and getting change. Take a seat in the living room. I will be right down.'

I sense I am rushing her to prepare for her night out. 'It is a quick chat. Nothing important.'

While she runs upstairs to finish changing, I walk around her living room, observing her choice of furniture, and eventually turn to her photos. I am intrigued if she has a boyfriend and what her parents look like. There is no sign of a relationship and her parents appear naturally happy in her holiday pictures at a snow resort and a beach. She appears happy go luck in her pictures. I do not see siblings and assume she is a lonely child.

Rachael finally comes back and startles me. 'Hey, admiring my photos. Sorry to make you jump. So, why are you?'

I get flustered, like they have caught me doing something I shouldn't. 'Huh. Yeah. I am going away for a month. Nothing special. Just a business trip. I was wondering if you could monitor my place. During your natural routine.'

It surprised Rachael; I only came round to tell her that, 'No problem. What are you doing?'

I do not want to bore her with the details, 'Just helping someone sort out their business. Boring stuff.'

Rachael still wants to hear about her. 'What kind of business?'

I continue to play it down, 'A small paper company. Old money. Seem to struggle with the times.'

Rachael continues to delve into my working life. 'You never told me what you do exactly.'

I feel overwhelmed to go into more detail. 'It is boring stuff. I don't want to give you the impression I am dull.'

Rachael smiles and finds me humorous. 'You don't look like a boring guy. You drive a Mercedes Benz and you wear lavish suits. A hot shot lawyer.'

I laugh off her compliments. 'No. I count money all day.'

Rachael guesses, 'Huh. A stock broker. Or a banker.'

I always get the wrong answer, 'An accountant. But give advice on how to spend their money and save on expenses. Also, touch on tax breaks.'

Racheal is not bored. 'How much could you save me if you looked into my business?'

I have to make a hazard guess, 'You probably make over a hundred thousand with the type of clients you may have. Your costs will be software, drawing equipment and traveling expenses. So, your profit is roughly 40% of turnover, which is $40,000. That is a tax bill of $7,606 at 22%. If you are a limited company, which is more likely, then tax is $8,400. at 21%. But, with a salary of $9,950 added to your expenses, the tax will drop to $6,6310.50 minimum. You then add other expenses you can claim. I can get your tax down to around $3,000.'

Rachael's eyes almost pop out with my accuracy. 'I can see why you have a nice car and nice clothes. My tax last year was actually $10,000 and yes, I am a corporate business. Would you take over my tax affairs?'

I truly do not need the extra work, but I feel obliged. 'I will pop over when I get back. For the time being, you can get your receipts together and I will analyze your business.'

Thirty minutes later, I find myself with another client, which happens. I wonder if she could be my type to settle down with, but keep forgetting my thoughts about my assessment of her.

And Her

♥

It is late afternoon on Saturday.

A woman by the name of Skyla Parker shares an apartment with her long-term boyfriend in Los Angeles. It is her boyfriend's birthday, and she plans a surprised party for his thirtieth.

Skyla holds the gathering at their place and has brought home party food from the local supermarket to put in the oven. She ordered a cake with his name and age in the shape of a golf ball and can feed up to twenty people on a cake stand. She invited only fifteen of their close friends.

The guests have already arrived and waiting for her boyfriend to come back from having a birthday drinks with a friend at a golf country club. Emily has also brought in soft drinks, alcohol, including prosecco and plastic cups to make a toast for later. She makes sure they each have a cup and their chosen drink.

I set everything for when he comes home.

Skyla is Caucasian, with long flowing blonde hair down to her shoulder, and is in her thirties already. She is five foot six with a slim, athletic figure with curves in the right place. Her eyes are dark brown with a narrow face and high cheekbones.

Her friends would say she is an extrovert with an outgoing personality. She enjoys going to the gym doing cardio exercises.

The clothes she wears are dresses which are knee-length, which are simple in design with no frilly attachments. Her shoes are designer heels as an expression of how hard she has worked to earn her salary.

Reaching thirty-five, the idea of wanting children is now at the forefront of her mind. Two children would be ideal for her and preferably a boy and a girl. Her biological clock is telling her she wants to be married and try for kids in the next year.

Skyla has been together with her partner for five years and engaged for two years. She has been wondering when they will set the date and plan for the wedding.

Her fiance is Brad Chandler.

Her career is an Investment Analyst for an investment company in Wall Street. There is a rumor of an opening for a management position. She thinks there could be one other person interested in the position.

Brad is Caucasian and six feet tall with a muscular frame, like an American football player. He has brown hair and piercing blue eyes with a square jaw. He is clean shaven with fair skin.

His clothes are casual trousers with a plain shirt and leather loafers to feel comfortable and relax easier after a stressful day at work.

He is an extrovert who enjoys socializing week nights, drinking with friends and meeting up with other couples for dinner and drinks on the weekends.

For work, he is a fund manager for a company similar to his girlfriend, but he oversees pensions and makes important investment decisions.

The couple live in 'Windsor at Hancock Park Apartments' in 445 North Rossmore Avenue near Larchmont Village, a quaint old town. They have nearby amenities including shopping mall, restaurants and bars. It is next to the 'Wiltshire Country Club', which is the main reason they lived here. Brad loves playing golf, and it is right next door.

Brad and his friend are sharing a bottle of white wine and observing the women golfers coming and going in the bar. All the ladies are tall and tanned with nothing else to do except socialize with their girlfriends.

Brad is pondering on his life, 'Mike, have you ever woke up one day and realize where you want to be?'

Mike laughs at him. 'Every time I drown myself in a bottle of wine. Why are you thinking this now?'

Brad stairs into his wine as he replies, 'One minute I am loving the hustle and bustle of work and the social life that comes with it. Then suddenly I don't want that anymore. I'm tired of letting life go by. I think I am ready to settle down now.'

Mike laughs again. 'Thats why you have a gorgeous girl-friend at home. You are a lucky SOB to have someone like Skyla. She is attractive and acts like a secretary to you. You don't have to plan your life. She will do anything for you.'

Brad does not seem to appreciate it. 'Yeah, but you only see that. I think I want what you have. A woman with an opinion. I love the way you two argue. It is constructive and you laugh about it.'

Mike's facial expression changes from being amused to a worry concern. 'You're not telling me you are thinking of breaking up with her? Right?'

Brad struggles to hide his thoughts. 'I don't see Skyla as a marrying type. I think my family will see her as an airhead. All my friends and her friends think she is great if you want a laugh and menial conversation. But, if you have a problem, she is the last person any of her friends would go to. And Skyla would be the last person to know. I don't want a wife like her. One time, a really close friend of hers, who I have a fondness for, had a health scare. I knew nothing about it. I asked her if she told Skyla. You know what she said.'

Mike has a blank expression. 'What?'

Brad continues, 'She said, "Why would I tell her? She isn't interested in the serious issues."'

Mike cannot believe what he is hearing. 'What will you do about your relationship? I mean, are you going to have a talk?'

Brad has a more drastic idea. 'I am going to end it. Then ask her to move out of the apartment. I realize what I want and I am going to find her.'

Mike doesn't know if he needs to do that. 'You know I am on your side and here for you. But why don't you speak to Skyla about this? She may not realize her friends cannot approach her. Have you asked Skyla if she is interested in her friends' personal lives?'

Brad ignores his question. 'I know everything about her. So, I do not need to ask her if she is unaware of her selfishness .'Mike can see he has already made his mind up. ' When are you going to tell her?'

Brad has been thinking about ending the relationship for a few months. 'Today. Someone is making plans for my birthday at her place.'

Mike almost sprays out his wine out of his mouth. 'What?'

Brad goes coy. 'I have kind of been confiding in someone about our relationship. It kind of went from there.'

Mike takes a guess. 'It's someone from our office. Kathy in accounts?'

Brad laughs, 'No. She has that annoying laugh.'

Mike is curious now, 'Then who?'

Brad glances around the room as if someone could listen to their conversation and whispers, 'Rachael.'

Mike is open-mouthed, 'Rachael in marketing?'

Brad confirms, 'Yeah.'

Mike wonders how they met, 'But she never comes into our office. How did you get together?'

Brad goes into detail, 'We got chatting at the vending machine. We were getting coffee. Her office is across the way from the vending machine. Well, one day we went to push the same button. Our hands touched and awkwardly fumbled, which sparked a conversation.'

Mike has no surprise. 'Thats convenient. Her desk was within cyc level of the vending machine. She obviously clocked you and waited for you to get your regular hit of espresso. There was no coincidence.'

Brad behaves as if it was fate. 'It was timing. I felt I needed someone to talk to, and she was there.'

Mike has his own ideas, 'And suddenly your stars aligned. You already checked out of the relationship and used her as an escape. Do you plan on telling her about the other woman?'

Brad had not seen this through properly. 'Of course not. She will never cross paths with Rachael. And I don't want a drawn out break up. After tonight, I will leave it a week and tell her next Friday.'

Skyla is getting anxious as she checks the time, expecting him to be back from the golf club by five o'clock. It is now close to half past. To calm her nerves, one of her friends and co-worker called Carla makes conversation.

Skyla welcomes the distraction. 'Work is fine. There's could be a new position going to work. Hoping I can go for the role. It will mean a ten percent pay rise with a higher commission. I really want the job. But the other girl is talented.'

Carla meant her relationship. 'How are you and Brad?'

Skyla a puzzled frown. 'How do you mean?'

Carla is aware of her want of having children. 'Have you spoken to Brad yet about you want to take the relationship to the next level?'

Skyla laughs off the question, 'No. It is not like I want kids tomorrow. I have been thinking about us a lot and I think I am ready to settle down. But, he has been busy with working later than usual over the last few months. There has not been a right time to have the talk. By the time the weekend comes along, we are busy seeing our friends and you.'

Carla rubs her arm. 'Make the time. How do you think he will react?'

Skyla is not sure of the question. 'How do you mean? We are engaged, dah.'

Carla is more forward. 'Do you think he really wants to settle down? He is out most week nights.'

Skyla ignores her opinion. 'My family will love him when they eventually meet him. My friends see him as a catch and we have fun together.'

Carla gives up on trying to tell her Brad is having second thoughts about their relationship.

One of her guests has been watching for Brad to come back. Her guest shrieks, saying he is coming. She shouts at everyone, saying he is on his way up.

Skyla tells everyone to find a place in the room to hide and come out when she gives the go ahead. Everyone rushes round to find a place to conceal themselves and be quiet. You can hear a pin drop now.

Brad enters the elevator and wonders how he was going to break it off gently with Skyla. Then finding an excuse to spend his birthday with Rachael instead. Before going round to his new lover, he has to ask Skyla to move out of his apartment by the end of Sunday. The door to the elevator opens as he prepares to give Skyla the bad news.While he takes out his apartment key, his nerves kick in and worried Skyla will make a scene and drag her heels moving out. He has butterflies in his stomach as he opens the door and prepares to tell her.He does not know Skyla has planned a home birthday surprise.

The guests and Skyla hear the door lock click and prepare to jump out and surprise Brad. Skyla quickly rushes to the door to greet him before their friends show their faces.

It startles Brad when he sees Skyla at the door. 'You scared me. Whats up?'

Skyla gives him a big smile. 'Did you enjoy your drinks with Mike?'

Brad suspects her overly smile while he walks into his apartment. 'What is going on? Please tell me you have not made plans. I have made plans to go out with Pete and Dave and a few other guys for drinks.'

Skyla does not pick on the fact that they are a part of a birthday celebration. 'I thought I would organize a surprise party for your thirtieth.'

Brad goes cold, 'Please don't tell me you organize something. You normally tell me if you have made plans.'

Without warning, all the guests jump out from their hiding places and shout surprise, which scares the life out of Brad. He embarrassingly waves at their friends and quietly takes Skyla out of the apartment and partially closes the door, to have a quiet word with Skyla.

Skyla wonders why he is acting strange. 'Our friends are inside. They have come here for us. You.'

Brad realizes this will be harder to end the relationship. 'I thought it was going to be just the two of us. But, I can't wait for a right time. Skyla, I don't want to be with you anymore. You're not marriage material. You're a great girlfriend who is up for a laugh and makes menial conversation. But I am ready to move on to find a wife. I want a wife on a deep, meaningful level. Someone who I can proudly introduce to my parents. I don't just want a hot wife. I want someone who cares about other people and not in airy fairy non sense. Also, I want you to move out before Monday. I'm turning thirty and realize what it is I want in life.'

Skyla is speechless, dumbfounded by what she is hearing. 'I thought we were ready to move on to the next level with me. We are engaged. I can be that person who cares about other people. I mean, I care about other people. I can make menial conversations. We are great together.'

Brad feels awkward and sorry for her. 'You didn't know Ellie, one of your close friends, had a health scare. Until I told you about it. All we talk about is work and television shows.'

Skyla tears up as her world is falling apart. Brad is not sure how to deal with their friends and takes the easiest way out. He walks off, leaving Skyla to explain why there was no surprise party.Skyla cries while watching Brad walk away and struggles to understand how their relationship finished.

Their guests are wondering why both of them have not come into the apartment yet. Carla goes outside to see what is happening. Carla soon realizes Brad is not coming in, and Skyla is upset. All she can do is comfort her and let her friend cry on her shoulder. Skyla cannot face hers and Brad's friends and so Carla goes back inside and explains the party is not happening. Nothing sufficiently explained and the guests quietly leave without asking questions. When the guests were gone, Carla stays with Skyla to keep her company and eventually gather her belongings.

It was Sunday morning at seven o'clock, and Skyla wakes up from sleeping on the sofa. Carla stayed with her until she fell asleep and found a blanket to put over her.Carla offered to come back tomorrow to help her pack her things and drive her to another apartment. Carla is Caucasian, with neck length brunette hair and similar age to Skyla. Her height is five foot six, with a slim build and pale skin. She has a slim, oblong face with brown eyes. Works in the same company in marketing.

She has time for her friends, a good listener, and offers her thoughts on discussion. She is married with two young kids and likes to stay out of other people's business unless asked.Skyla temporarily forgets she is no longer with Brad. She stares at her engagement ring and does not want to take it off. Watching the diamond glisten in the light while she wonders what she is going to do with the rest of her life. All she has left is her career, which is not enough to keep her happy. A friend she has known since college manages holiday homes for people visiting Los Angeles and making business trips.

She has to ask her friend for a favor, as she has to wait until she gets her next paycheck as she has maxed out her credit card.Luckily for her, he has a place which he says is empty for a month and allows her to stay there until it is unavailable.In the meantime, she will search for her own place and allow time to find a deposit. She can move into the villa today.

The property is a two-bed villa with a master bedroom. There is an open, plain dining area and a living area with a separate kitchen. It has a communal double shower and standalone bath.There is a swimming pool and a barbeque area with patio table and four chairs.It is perfect for her as she is a forty-minute journey to work using the subway.

Clare comes back after nine o'clock to help Skyla pack her clothes and any ornaments she owns. It takes all of one hour to gather her belongings and only five minutes to load it in Clara's car.When Skyla is ready to leave, Clara gives her time alone to spend in the apartment, believe they leave for the villa.Skyla takes one long last stare at her home of four and a half years. As she wonders around going in each room, she remembers the good times she had with Brad. It makes her tearful again, as if she is mourning his death. She holds on to the engagement ring so she can feel he is near her.After a few moments of walking around the empty apartment, Skyla leaves the key on the coffee table in the living room. Then walks out of the front door one last time.

Carla watches her friend get into her car and squeeze her hand before starting the car. She drives away slowly while Skyla rests her head against the door window and stare into space.

During the drive to her new place, Carla asks her what went wrong. Skyla does not know herself.

Carla keeps to the city limit while checking her mirrors. 'What excuse did Brad give you to want to end it?'

Skyla thinks back to her conversation she had yesterday with him. 'He said that he is ready to find a wife. I did not show enough caring. He wants to meet a wife who does not talk about work and television shows.'

Carla is confused. 'But you were engaged to be married. He had been with you for five years. He already knew what you were like before getting engaged. It was him who was eager to marry you.'

Skyla is confused herself. 'Exactly. I didn't force him to want to marry me.'

Carla says nothing more, as Skyla does not want to keep talking about why he broke up with her. They drive for another six-minutes before reaching the villa.

When they arrive just after 10.30, Carla cannot believe how nice her place is. She thinks it is better than Brad's apartment. Skyla is too consumed with her predicament to show interest in her temporary home.

They both leave her boxes in the main bedroom for Skyla to sort out in her own time. Carla only stays for about ten minutes as she has made plans to go out with her husband tonight.

Skyla changes into her two-piece swimming costume to go for a swim and bathe topless for the rest of the day.She uses the time to process what has happened in the last twelve hours.

A Misunderstanding

It is Sunday morning after eleven o'clock. My taxi has arrived to take me to 'New York Private Jet Rentals & Charters' at 118 W 114th St #1W, New York. My five employees are each finding their way to the airport and ask them to keep the receipts for their taxis, so I can claim the cost against my firm.

My employees are Mark, Caroline, Jessica, Simon and Alina. They have worked for me over several years with transferrable skills to analyze any industry business.

Mark is Caucasian, in his thirties and five foot eight. His frame is slim and stocky build. He has short dark brown hair with a side parting.

His suits are two pieces and dark corporate colors, as are his ties with white shirts.

He is single and career focused, hoping to one day manage a large project like the one we are going to turn around.

I made him a manager of the junior accountants.

Caroline is Caucasian, in her forties and six feet tall. She is slim with long strawberry straight hair that falls below her shoulder.

Her work clothes are suit trousers and blouse with a suit jacket.

She is married with two children and works to live and is happy with her current stage in life with her husband.

I employ her as a management accountant to analyze manufacturing companies.

Jessica is a black African American, in her early twenties and five foot six. She has a curvaceous frame with straighten afro hair in a bob.

Her work clothes are knee-length skirts with a matching jacket and blouse.

She is single and begins her career in accountancy as a junior to assist the team and deal with ad hoc work.

I have her take care of the mundane stuff like checking the financial transactions, such as expenses, are recording accurately and the suppliers are genuine.

Simon is Asian, six feet tall and in his fifties. He is filling out with a paunch and black hair.

His two-piece suits are a little bigger than his frame and wears his ties with his top button undone on his shirts.

He is married with three children and has reached a point in his career where is ready to slow down. Spend more time with his wife and family.

I ask him to manage the firm and lead the team to carry out analyzing our clients' assets such as buildings, intellectual property and goodwill.

Alina is a black African American, five foot six and in her late twenties. She has a slim body with an athletic build and has long straightened afro hair down to her shoulder.

Her suits are trousers and a shirt with a waistcoat.

She has a long-term boyfriend and no kids.

I have her work with Jessica and together plow through the checks.

During our six-hour flight, Mark, Jessica and Alina take advantage of the wines on board the plane. Behaving like they are children in a sweet shop. Caroline and Simon have their mind on home and missing their family. They hope the work will finish in less than a month.I watch a film on my cell phone through a streaming service. I have a couple I subscribe to. One film I like to watch is a romance film called You've Got Mail.

When we arc less than half an away, Mark comes and sits opposite me to talk about our new project.

Mark is trying to be professional while tipsy. 'I would like to lead this one. Come up with a solution to turn the company around.'

I think he has quite a way to go still. 'Simon is going to run shot gun on this. You need a couple of more going concern companies under your belt.'

Mark disagrees, but there is nothing he can say to convince me.

Once we land in Los Angeles at 'Los Angeles Private Jet Charter - Travel King International', I arrange for two taxi taking us to their hotel and my house.

I have organized for my employees to stay at the "Beverly Wilshire Hotel" along Wilshire Boulevard road. Their rooms are on the same floor, so they work together in the hotel. My accommodation is at "The Melrose Villa" between North Edinburgh Avenue and North Heyworth Avenue, behind Pali-hotel Melrose Avenue" It is a three-bedroom villa with its own swimming pool and very spacious.

The taxi driver stops right outside the villa and he helps to get my luggage out of the trunk and leave them on the sidewalk. Once I pay him the fare, I take my time walking in.

The photos on the internet do not do it justice. The master bedroom has a kingsize bed with a chrome metal four post frame. It could tempt me to buy it and have it as an owned weekend break.

I go into the bathroom to compare it to the pictures on the website. It could fit four people in the shower room. The bathtub is free standing and made of porcelain. They tiled the floor and walls in white and gray marble.

When I go to see the kitchen, I hear a splash outside and wonder if it is a stray animal helping themselves to the pool. I assume it is a dog and go outside to shoo it away.

There is nothing there, except for the pool water rippling. For a moment, I think the place is haunting. As I walk back inside, I see a shadow on the ground coming towards me and I jump. A person belonging to the shadow comes from around the corner and shrieks while covering her chest. I end up stumbling backwards and trip inside the door entrance and fall on my back. The scream continues and eventually realizes it is a woman's voice.

The topless woman with a towel around her screams at me, 'I'm going to call the cops!'

I pick myself up and check if I have damaged my thousand dollar suit. 'Do I look like a burglar?'

She is too hysterical to hear me. 'What did you say?'

I repeat myself, 'I am not a burglar.'

She eventually calms down. 'What are you doing here?'

I watch her adjusting her towel and scratching her neck. 'I booked this place for a month.'

She is deep in thought. 'What?'

I give up, 'Put some clothes on. I will not mug you. And you're not my type. I bought this place for a month. What is your excuse?'

The woman disagrees. 'A friend is allowing me to stay here. He manages the property.'

I assume she is staying here for free while I am paying for this place. 'I will get hold of the manager's number and call him.'

The woman realizes how serious I am. 'You don't have the number? I thought you booked this place?'

I explain who booked it. 'I had my secretary find this place and call them.'

The woman offers to contact him. 'I will call him.'

We wait for him to arrive and in the meantime; she changes out of her swimming costume and into her clothes. I stay by the pool to give her privacy while waiting for the manager to clear this problem up.

I should have stayed at the hotel.

The manager finally arrives a little after eight o'clock and wants to relax before tomorrow.

I pictured a guy wearing scruffy jeans and a shirt with a cigarette in his mouth. But he is wearing a suit and clean shaven. I can see it embarrassed him as he realizes he forgot she was here.

I double check with my secretary booking the place. 'You see my name having this place over the next month?'

The man confirms, 'I'm sorry, Skyla. I completely forgot I booked it out.'

I know her name now. 'Is there another accommodation you can put her in? Clearly, she has nowhere else to go.'

Skyla is too proud to accept charity. 'It's okay. I will find somewhere else to stay. I wanted somewhere quick.'

She is stressing that she will pay for another place to stay.

The man shows a surprise. 'You pay for another place?'

I insist, 'You have my card details. Put it on my tab.'

Skyla will not accept my charity. 'I do not need your money. Jack, I will pay this time. Can you find me another place I can stay at?'

Jack has no other spare vacancy. 'I'm sorry. I can't help you out.'

I still want to help. 'I'll pay you two thousand dollars find a place. You can use the limo to carry your things.'

Skyla is stunned and embarrassed now. 'Please. I am not a charity.'

I can see I tempted him. 'I can add another thousand.'

Skyla goes shy, 'No. Now, you are embarrassing me.'

I can see I am making her uncomfortable. 'Jack, can you leave us for a moment?'

Jack can see how awkward this is getting and understands as he gives us space.

Skyla slumps on the armchair of the sofa. 'I have nowhere else to go. I have no money for a deposit until I next get paid. Which is in two weeks' time.'I feel sorry for her as she sits there upset. 'Stay here until you can find your own apartment. I will tell Jack.'

Skyla struggles to make eye contact, puts her hand out to shake mine. 'Thank you.'

I realize I did not introduce myself. 'By the way, the name's Lewis. Richard Lewis. And you are Skyla.'

Skyla gives me her full name. 'Skyla Parker.'

After Jack leaves, the next question, who is sleeping where? I assume she has already chosen her room and hope it is not the master bedroom.I ask, 'Have you already chosen a room?'

Skyla has not. 'My first day here. I have not unpacked yet. I thought I would go for a swim first.'I am cheeky. 'Do you always go topless swimming?'

Skyla breaks a smile. 'I was also sunbathing.'

I suggest we eat first. 'You must be hungry. We will eat first and then unpack afterwards.'

When dinner arrives, I take out a couple of plates and cutlery to eat at the table. Skyla takes the food into the livingroom, but I prefer eating at the table.

Skyla wonders why I am staring at her in a funny way. 'Why are you not coming into the living room? I want to watch "The Blacklist".'

I am quite forward, 'In my house, we eat at the table. We do not watch television while having dinner. If you were paying, you could eat anywhere you want. For now, we eat at the table.'

Skyla roles her eyes at me. 'Okay. Okay.'

During dinner, she has some questions she wants to ask me.

Skyla has no filter and just comes out with it. 'So, how rich are you?'

I scoff and vaguely with the answer, 'Rich enough.'

Skyla is curious about the way I dress. 'What is it you do exactly? You are obviously not a supervisor or work for someone.'

I swipe my mouth with a serviette. 'I count money all day.'

Skyla clicks her fingers to come up with a guess, which I know she will get wrong like everyone else. 'You're an accountant.'

I cannot believe she is the first to guess right. 'Yes. That is correct. What gave me away? Whenever I tell someone that, they go straight for the stockbroker or banker.'

Skyla smiles and gloats. 'I know a lot of stockbrokers and bankers. And you don't fit the bill. I'm an investment analyst. I work with stockbrokers and bankers.'

I am curious, 'Dated a lot of brokers and bankers?'

Skyla goes quiet. 'I dated one. And, I work with a lot of them. I'm an investment analyst at the LA stock exchange.' I joke with her. 'Are you a fan of "Wall Street"? See yourself as Gordon Gekko, hmm.'

Skyla smiles and almost laughs. 'Something like that. This is not so bad, eating at the table.'

She almost gets a smile out of me, but I contain myself, and we finish our meal.

First For Everything

♥

The next day, I get woken up by a loud machine and realize it is the noise of a blender rattling in my ear. At first, I wonder who is making that noise, thinking I am at home. Then I remember meeting Skyla last night, and it was her making all the noise. It reminds me I will have to make small talk with her until she leaves. It could take her a up to two weeks to find an apartment and move in.

I check my clock to see if it is close to my usual time of waking up. It is gone six o'clock and I do not get out of bed any earlier than eight o'clock. Being your own boss has its perks when you can go into work anytime you feel like.

I jump in the shower and do not realize I have not locked the door. I decide to go for a long shower.Skyla remembers to hang her towel in the bathroom and sees the door is unlocked. She walks in, not realizing Richard is having a shower. Richard is does not know she has seen him completely naked.Skyla quickly leaves before she is seen and closes the door behind her. She giggles to herself with embarrassment. Seeing his phallus has shocked her as she has never seen his size before. Which leaves her behaving like a schoolgirl.After I finish washing myself, I wonder if I will see Skyla before she goes to work. It is coming up to 07.15 by the time I finish dressing in my suit and being ready to leave for work.

Skyla woke up at 05.30 to get ready and leave for 07.30 to go to work. The Hollywood Stock Exchange 1925 Century Park East is where she gets in 08.00. She has her daily board meeting discussing markets to go into and be aware of new unstable countries. She does not finish work until six o'clock.

Her role at the company she works for is research and evaluating new companies in low-risk countries and market to predict its future performance and determine its suitability to a specific investor. Being an investment analyst also involves creating an overall financial strategy to the people who trade on the floor, in the pit.

She loves her work and is very good at it. She has been at her company for ten years now. The money gives her mobility to enjoy life and live in comfort. All she wants now is to marry and have children. She thought Brad was that guy. Skyla has doubt whether she will ever meet another man who can give her what she wants. Wonders if Brad has lost her confidence in men. She is worried her chance of happiness was only with Brad.

Once I am ready, wearing one of my two thousand dollar suits, I feel prepared for what today brings and meeting my client at his office. I will meet my work colleagues first at 09.00 in the hotel lobby for coffee before dealing with the mess.

When I go into the kitchen, I was pleasantly surprised to see Skyla in a silvery blue tailored dress. Her hair tied back in a bun. She differs totally from the woman I met yesterday in a two-piece bathing suit with long wet flowing hair. It is like I have met her twin sister.

Skyla smiles when she sees me. 'Morning. I hope I made little noise. Sleep okay?'

I watch her drinking a green concoction of a smoothie. 'Is that nice?'

Skyla takes a big gulp before answering. 'Yep. It gives me a boost before I get into work. Want some?'

I do not find the appearance overly nice. 'No thanks. I will have some toast and latte. You want a coffee?'

Skyla watches me walking over to the coffee machine. 'No thanks. I am going to drink my smoothie by the pool before I go to work.'

I will join her when I get my breakfast. 'See you out there.'

When I go outside, I wonder where she is and walk around the corner to see her sat reading a magazine.

I still cannot believe she is wearing a suit. 'Are you off somewhere interesting?'

Skyla laughs, even though I was not trying to be funny. 'This is how I go to work?'

I find her curious and wonder what her job entails. 'What do you do as an investment analyst? Advise to buy low and sell high?'

Skyla fakes a laugh this time. 'Very funny. I collect information, perform research, and analyze assets, such as stocks, bonds, currencies, and commodities. '

I cannot believe she is both intelligent and attractive. 'Got any stock tips? I could do with some money.'

Skyla is not sure if I am joking and ignores the question, 'What do you do for a living?'

I take a sip of coffee when she asks me, 'Excuse me. I prevent companies from going into liquidation.'

Skyla is keen to know what that involves. 'So, how do you stop a company from going bust?'

I find a simple way of explaining without the boring details, 'I analyze their assets and expenses. Then help them cut costs without making employees redundant. Then find money to modernize their production, IT equipment and how best practice monitoring financial performance.'

Skyla is fascinated by my work. 'Wow. What kind of companies?'

I use my current project as an example, 'Well, at the moment I have a newspaper company who is behind the times. Still printing paper and no online presence.'

Skyla has a look of shock. 'You're kidding. In this day and age. How much will it cost to save the company?'

I take another sip of coffee. 'Looking at around five hundred million dollars.'

Skyla almost spills her drink out of her mouth. 'Five hundred million dollars? Wow! How do you find that kind of money?'

I casually explain, 'I find people who have that kind of money. Including merchant banks? What does your work entail?'

Skyla flicks her hand to imply her work was easy. 'Nothing as complicated as yours. I just assess risk tolerance before advising to invest in a certain market. Factor in economy, potential wars and disasters. Then consider how many funds are available to invest from the company clients' money. I have to factor also in the sunk costs such as legal fees, commissions and whether my advisor fees make it cost effective.'

I find her work more interesting. 'How much money are we talking?'

Skyla throws a number in the air. 'Looking at funds of like two billion dollars. We have clients like oil billionaires and tech companies. How much do you charge for your services?'

I give her a ballpark figure. 'For this project, my client gets a bargain fee of around twenty million dollars. Also, commission from the lenders of a further five million. Looking at a turnaround of about month.'

Skyla is open-mouthed. 'You must be great at your job. I'm in the wrong business. How much is your firm worth?'

I try to keep a straight face when I tell her, 'We try to keep a cash flow of around fifty million dollars. The firm is worth around two hundred million with money tied in various property, low-risk companies and bonds.'

Skyla is lost for words. 'So, you are a millionaire. And, on that note, I am going into work.'

I think the same as her, 'I need to leave too. Will I see you tonight? Have dinner together? Thinking of using the barbeque.'

Skyla likes the idea of that. 'Thats a date. I mean, that sounds great.'

I stand up as she moves out of her chair and smile at her comment. 'It is an appointment. Have a nice day and I will see you tonight.'

Once she is gone, I arrange for a limousine to pick me up and then pick my co-workers up from the hotel.

Skyla's morning meeting finishes and her boss ask her and another female co-worker to stay behind. Skyla hopes the rumor about a position opening is true. She is confident her boss is going to mention about the management role. There should be no other reason he would ask the both of them to stay behind.

Her boss is in his fifties and wears expensive suits with a corporate tie and a white shirt. There is an offer of promotion he wants to announce.

Skyla pretends to be surprised. 'What is it?'

Her boss mentions the role, 'The senior manager is looking to leave for pastures new. Change of scenery. I think it will suit one of you for the position.'

The other woman is confident she will get it, 'I would be glad to resume the role. I have been here six glorious years. I get on with everyone, and my track record is unblemished.'

Skyla fights her corner. 'I have been here for ten years and I have the same tracked record, if not better.'

Her boss finds them both amusing and likes their keenness. 'Well, do what you two are good at. I will make my decision at the end of the month. Now, go to work.'

When I arrive at the hotel, my team is already in the lobby in the waiting area that has chairs for guests to relax.

They stand up when they see me and I suggest we go for coffee before heading into our meeting at ten o'clock.

While we have our coffees and teas, I discuss what our work will entail. I list several key areas we will focus on cutting costs. I also tell them I have a suspicion someone in the company is stealing money. So, we will have to focus on the high value numbers such as cost of sales and repair and renewals.

I tell each person what I want them to do. 'Simon, I want you to confirm the asset values on the balance sheet. Check to see if they have undervalued anything to give the impression of the company facing financial trouble. Caroline, you check for any problems in production that could cause costs to spiral out of control. Jessica and Alina look for any fraudulent activities that could have caused the company to end up where it is today. Include verifying all the suppliers to see they are legit and not made up. Mark, I want you to summarize what Jessica and Alina find. Is everyone happy with their responsibilities?'

Caroline has an idea of where to focus. 'I will check their budgets and compare to actual costs. See if their budges are unrealistic. Therefore, throwing ridiculous over spending.'

Simon has a few things he wants to explore. 'I will check to see when the last the time the company assets were revalued. See if the building and goodwill have gone up in value. They may be worth more and be able to offset against borrowings .'The others have nothing to add and so our meeting finishes, we all go in the limousine to meet our new client.The first day at the newspaper company was gathering a list of the suppliers, assets owned, list of expenses on the income statement, and a year's worth of bank statements.

This alone was a day's work and preparing spreadsheets to record the data and values. The owner was busy and delegated a senior manager to give us the information we need.

It is five o'clock when I decide to go back to the villa and relax for the evening. The limousine takes me back and then returns to take my people back to the hotel.

When I arrive back, I take my suit jacket off and tie. I undo my top button and roll my sleeves up.

I go into the kitchen to find an apron to wear before I go to fire up the gas barbeque.The grill is already clean and so I do not have to prepare it and fire it up. While it warms up, I take one packet of sausage and burger from the fridge and place on the grill.When the food is cooking, I prepare a salad with dressing and as I go to take the bowl outside; I hear Skyla coming in. I continue to go outside and finish preparing the patio table with plates and cutlery, including a bottle of cold crisp Rose.Skyla finally appears after changing into casual clothes, wearing jean shorts and a vest. She appears exhausted. I think she has been crying.I stand by the table, uncorking the bottle of wine. 'Hi. Just cooking sausages and burgers. Have made a bowl of salad.'

Skyla appreciates my effort. 'Where did you find the apron and do you always wear suits for cooking?'

I laugh at her humor. 'I only brought suits with me and I found the apron in one of the kitchen draws. The print on the apron of a woman in a bikini was appropriate for the pool.

Skyla laughs at my sense of humor. 'Very sexy. Can you pour me out a drink? I need after the day I have had. I brought some beers from the liquor store. Kind of getting bored with the wine and champagne you keep.'

I wave my hand at her. 'No problem. Take a seat and you can tell me all about your day.'

After we finish eating and switch to drinking beer, we get to know each other for the first time. I allow Skyla to go first asking her to give me some knowledge of growing up and how she came to be staying here.Skyla thinks back as far as college, 'I found I was great at maths and studied economics and finance. I told myself that when I finish, I will go traveling for a year or two before finding a career. I was all prepared to go and took a job to save up during the summer. It was where I am now, as an admin. I got on with everyone and they offered me a job in the end. They had my CV and knew admin was not my limit. I bottled going traveling thinking I would not get an opportunity like this again. Once I found my perfect job, I met a guy called Brad. We met at a bar where all the financial workers go. We got engaged. I loved him and I saw myself having kids with him. Then two days ago, I organized a surprise thirtieth, and he dumps me.'

Skyla briefly laughs and wipes a tear away, and I can see it completely broke her. I can feel her pain from where I am sitting. She asks about my life.

I tell her my short story. 'When I finished college, I worked for a practice firm and qualified as a CPA. Then, after a few more years, I went alone and gradually built up my firm. I had a couple of good breaks through word of mouth and ended up where I am now.'Skyla is curious about my personal life. 'Is there a Misses Lewis?'

I smile mainly through embarrassment. 'I never found the opportunity to meet anyone. I was too busy working long hours seven days a week. Every social event was picking new clients. If chatted up a woman, it was to get my foot in the front door with no strings attached. I mean sex.'

Skyla giggles and smiles. 'I know what you meant. So, you not interested in being with someone? Rather chase the money?'I feel a nerve after what she said, 'No. I have always wanted to be with someone. But the opportunity never arose. I either stayed at home and feel sorry for myself or go out and make money.'

Skyla is shocked. 'You're a great-looking guy. You can have anyone you want. Why don't you find her now? You have made it already and have you people to run your business. Find her now.'I find the idea scary, 'I'm petrified. That this ideal woman does not exist. Then, the reality sinks in that I will be lonely for the rest of my life. By not looking, I can tell myself there is still hope. I can live on hope than face reality.'

Skyla seems to relate. 'Well, I thought Brad was my ideal man and thought he existed for me. But you have to keep going until you find your soul mate. Or else what are we living for?'

I admit my jealousy. 'I envy people who seem to fall out of bed and into a relationship. Like it is second nature. There is no hurdle. It is like they were sitting at home and they came knocking on their door. When I notice an amiable woman, they see through me and at the next guy. I have never had someone see me. Everyone tells me I deserve to be with someone and I am a great catch. But they seem to go for the bad boys who cannot afford a belt for their trousers.'Skyla tries to be optimistic. 'One day, she will see you. I promise.'I wonder what it is like to be in a relationship. 'Skyla, what's it like? Being with someone.'

Skyla tries to give her best description. 'It is like having a best friend. But with the intimacy. You can be yourself and wear your heart on your sleeves. You can let go of your deepest, darkest secrets and they won't tell a soul.'

Skyla wonders what it is like being wealthy. 'What is it like being rich?'I give her the truth, 'The notion of being rich does not make you happy. It only takes away one problem. It cannot buy love or friends. The money has no feelings or warmth to make you feel good about yourself. You can choose to kid yourself that money will buy something to give you happiness. But you only find happiness within. External factors do not give you that. When you see the rest of the world struggling, you quickly realize you are the odd one out. Being the only person with the money in your circle of friends makes life boring. Unless you pay for your friends to come on lavish holidays, you are alone.'

Skyla is taken aback. 'I never thought of being rich like that. I guess it takes you away from the ones you love.' We both learn a lot about each other tonight and I think it has allowed her to touch on her journey to move on.

I tell her I am here if she needs someone to listen to her. 'I know you are hurting. When you are ready to talk, I am here.'

Skyla really appreciates my offer. 'That means a lot to me. But my first protocol is to find my own apartment and move in before I get kicked out of this place.'

I decide I want to help. 'I can come with you. Help you find an apartment. When will you be searching?' Skyla welcomes my company. 'I would love that. The problem is, it is tomorrow. I know it is too short a notice. So, I am not expecting you to come.' I still want to help, 'I do own the company.'

Skyla's face lights up. 'Thank you.' I help her search for some apartments before we go to bed. Skyla notes down some addresses to begin with. Then, allow the realtor to guide her.

Apartment Hunting

♥

It is the next morning and we are both up having coffee together and she is having her morning smoothy again while I have with my latte. We discuss our plans today with her visit to the local estate agent nearby.

Last night, Skyla searched for realtors nearby dealing with lease agreement on apartments. She found one business called 'JMK Real Estate Service' and checked on their website. Their properties are priced between $1,800.00 and $2,400.00 per month. The property rental agency is at 145 South Fairfax Avenue. It is a fifteen-minute walk for us. But, I suggest using the limousine to drive to the properties.

Skyla scrolls through the website. 'There are only five properties available. They are on Glenhurst Avenue, Spaulding Avenue and Franklin Avenue. I also found another realtor called nVe at 639 N Fairfax Avenue, which is only a three-minute walk. Their prices are between $2,000.00 and 5,000.00.⫽

I ask her to show me her laptop, 'Right. I assume you earn $100,000 ball park with commission on top. So, you can afford conservatively thirty thousand dollars before taxes and other cost of livings. So, they are both in your price range.'

Skyla is annoyed about how I know her salary. 'Show off. You sure you want to come with me?'

I already cleared my day, 'I said I would, so lets get going.'

The limousine pulls up and we head to the cheaper price range at Fairfax Avenue. Once we arrive at the realtor, I allow Skyla to lead, as it is her finding a property to rent.

When we go inside, there is a man behind his desk staring at his desktop computer and we wait until he notices us standing in front of him. Once he notices us, his face lights up and he is happy to see us and quickly finds out what we are looking for.

Skyla mentions the five properties she saw on their website and the man tells us that Glenhurst Avenue is almost two hours away and so we squash that idea straight away. The other addresses are between four minutes and nineteen minutes away from the realtor. Skyla considers the forty minutes commute as the furthest she will travel. Her current commute time from the villa is the same.

Spaulding Avenue will take forty-two minutes and Franklin Avenue will be one hour. I advise her to only look at the Spaulding property. The rental cost there is $2,200. I give her a suggestion, 'If the property is not to your liking, we will go straight to nVe.'

Skyla is agreed, 'Let's do that.'

The man is content to accept our opinion and encourages us to look around. He offers to give us the keys to the property and trusts us, as our mode of transport is a limousine.

We arrive at the property by half past ten o'clock and we see the building is inset a few feet from the sidewalk and it is a row of apartments. The property has a flight of stairs leading up to the entrance. There are raised beddings left of the steps with planted flowers. The outside appears appealing.

Inside, the apartment is very light and airy, with white walls and wooden flooring.

I judge her expression of what she thinks of the place. 'Can you see yourself living here?'

Skyla peers out of the window to see the view. 'It is west Hollywood. The place is really nice, but I feel lost here and so far away from my friends.'

I instantly think it is not for her. 'Let's go back to the guy and say we will think about it. I know you don't want to live here.'

Skyla is surprised how much I can read her. 'I think I have been round you too long.'

We head back to the realtor.

After handing the key over, we go straight to nVe and see their availability.

When we arrive there, the woman at the desk shows us a brochure of the apartments while we wait for her help. The pictures of the internal apartments impress us and feel this is the right place for her. When she has finished with her admin work, she comes over to ask what we think of the pictures of the apartments. Skyla shows her enthusiasm and is keen to see inside the apartment.

Skyla has one main question. 'How much security deposit will I need?'

The woman is very courteous, 'We only ask for two months' rent and the standard security check.'

Skyla thinks of one other question.deposit? 'How soon can I move in once I pay the deposit? And how soon would you want the deposit?'

The woman is quite specific, 'You can move in the first week of August. In less than four weeks. This will allow time to check your references and you to make payment.'Skyla thinks about her finances. 'I can sort out a payment for the last week of July if you are happy with that?'

The woman is happy with her suggestion. 'That is totally fine. So long as the contract is signed by the third Friday of July.'Skyla wants to know about the references, 'Can I use a co-worker?

'The woman is fine with that. 'No problem. They can complete an electronic form we email a link to.'Once Skyla has finished having her questions answered, she takes us to one of the empty apartments, which is a showroom.

After initially showing us around the apartment, she leaves us the key to have a proper walk around.The woman assumes we are partners and says we make a great couple. We do not correct her and we ignore the comment.They fully furnished the show room to indicate how it will look once after moving in. The fittings are contemporary, so the rooms appear mo dern.It feels like a brand new apartment with a fragrance of new furniture. I can see in Skyla's face this is her new home. We mull over what she will initially need to buy when she moves in. In particular the bedroom and living area.The place is twice the footage as the last apartment we saw, and the views are more appealing.

Skyla is keen to sign the contract today to confirm she will move in. She gives the name, address and email of her friend Carla as a reference.I ask her opinion of the place and area in which she replies loving the whole setup. We hand back the key and go for something to eat for lunch.

By the time Skyla finishes completing the forms, it is near enough lunch time and I suggest finding a place to eat.

I remember seeing a food van outside when we arrived and suggest buying a sandwich roll there before heading back.W hile we wait in the queue, Skyla cannot stop getting excited about her new apartment and is grinning from ear to ear. Skyla continues to talk about how spacious and airy it is. She wishes she can move in now. She says how it reminds her of the Villa we are staying at and the price is affordable.

I am happy for her and while she is continuing with the fact that the building has a gym on the ground floor and a social area with tables and chairs.Skyla is eating and talking at the same time, and I notice she has mustard on her chin. She is oblivious as she continues to eat her roll. I cannot help using my serviette to dab her chin without her expecting it. It causes her to stop her conversation mid flow and is caught unaware.Our eyes lock while I wipe the sauce from her chin and soon after we both realize what we are doing, quickly look away. We both stare forward and we're not sure what to do. I find anything to spark conversation, such as the park across the road.Skyla clears her throat and joins in the conversation about the park being great for walks.For the first time, I notice she has dark brown eyes and tiny freckles across her nose. She has a cute nose.

Skyla freaks out as she thinks of Brad and hopes the moment does not give Richard any ideas. She is not interested in a rebound and has no intention of trying to find a new relati onship.We soon run out of conversation and all this shopping for rental apartments gets me thinking about my property in Beverly Hills. While I am in town, it would make sense to check the house over and is being managed properly. I would also like to show her the property as well.I ask her if she would like to see it. 'I have a property here. I want to go in and see it is okay.'

Skyla is surprised. 'You own a property here? Why didn't you stay at there rather than waste money paying rent?'

I will show her why. 'You will see when you get there.'

When we get back in the limousine, I ask the driver to take us to the name of a road. He enters it in a navigation system. We travel to 909 North Bedford Drive. It is a seventeen minute drive.

The driver slows down as we approach the house. I wait for Skyla's reaction when she sees a portion of the left side of the house above the gate. There is a wide and tall conifer bush above the height of the gate, obscuring the view of the property. We get out of the car and walk to the gate. After a few seconds, the gate opens and I lead us into the crescent moon shape drive. Skyla's face lights up when she sees how beautiful it is from the outside.

Skyla cannot believe the size of the house. 'This trumps my apartment. This confirms it. You are a millionaire.'

I take her inside through the front door. 'It is an investment. I have a huge mortgage on it. But I rent it out to studio bosses making wealthy drama films. I have an agreement with the studio to have it on demand. All the other times, it is empty. I often wonder if I could live in a house like this alone.'

Skyla is curious about my house in New York. 'Is your house as big as this?'

I describe my house. 'It is nowhere as big as this. My home is only a five bedrooms with a small garden. It is enough for me and does not feel too big. This house is eight bedrooms with six bathrooms. Too much for me. You can look around.'

We walk through the living area and kitchen before going upstairs. The size of both rooms blows her away.

I take her upstairs to view the bedrooms and ensuite. It takes about forty-five minutes to show her around. We finish in the master bedroom and stand by the window, overlooking the three acre garden. Skyla wonders why I brought the place. 'What made you buy the property?'

I bought it as an investment, 'There a movie company's looking for houses to film in. So, I bought it as a rental income. Hand it out to the likes of Paramount, MGM and Warner Brothers.'

Skyla cannot believe I rent out a mansion. 'You can move in here and find a wife.'

I almost laugh at the idea. 'This is too big for me. It will take me a week to find the wine cellar and a month to clean the house. And LA is not my home.'

Skyla rests her back against the wall. 'What is your ideal girl you want to marry?'

I never really thought about it. 'I want to meet a black woman who is around my age. She needs to have a career and be independent. I want to ensure my culture is remembered. How about you? Are you going to find another Brad?'

Skyla finds the question way too early. 'I want to get over Brad before I decide who my idea type is. Brad was my soul mate. It will take me forever to get over him.'I can see in her eyes how much Brad hurt her and I guess it could take her over a year to move on.

After I show her the house, we head back to the villa.

When we get back, I make a phone call to Simon to ask how today went with the client. While I talk to Simon, Skyla calls Carla about her being a reference to her new apartment.

Simon and the others are still compiling the list of suppliers and expense accounts before analyzing all the data.Simon gives me a brief breakdown. 'It has taken all day to record the information we are going to investigate. It will not be until tomorrow when we examine all suppliers, expense accounts and fix asset registrar.'

I will update our client, 'I will arrange a meetup with John and let him know how far we have got.'

Simon asks when I will find investors, 'When are you going to speak to your contacts? We will need around a hundred and fifty million dollars to improve their technology and make an overall on their machines. Based on today's costs.'

I have already considered several people and contacted them before coming to LA. 'I have arranged to meet up with them tomorrow night. I thought it would be a good idea to make it informal. Invite their wives and go to a restaurant. This is our biggest financial problem. The usual ten, twenty million from each investor will not be enough in this case..'

Simon asks if I will need him for the number crunching. 'Do you want me to provide the usual financial proposal to support the spending?'

I have built up a long-term trust with these people. 'They have dealt with me long enough. They will accept what I tell them.'

We hang up soon after, and Skyla has already finished her phone call.

We go outside while it is still daylight and sunny. Skyla appears agitated and wonders if her friend said no to being a reference.

I ask if everything is okay. 'Has your friend said she will do it?'

Skyla's face is white as a sheet. 'My mom texts me and I have a family get together. She wants to meet my fiance. I don't think I can face them, having to explain we are finished. The thought of everyone staring at me and giving a pity look.'I calm her down. 'Do you have to be there? Can you just say you have work?'

Skyla has to be there. 'I will be the only person not going. They will be suspicious. I wish I could go with someone to pretend to be my fiance.'

I make a suggestion, 'Do they know what color he is?'

Skyla has a puzzling frown. 'How do you mean?'

I give her an idea, 'I could pretend to be your fiance. If they don't know, he is white. Or come as a friend.'

Skyla takes a while to decide. 'Okay. Only if you are happy to do that.'I have no problem, 'It will be fine. When is it?'

Skyla gives me the day. 'Two weeks from this Saturday.'I will still be in town. 'Fine. No problem.'Skyla gets tearful. 'I'm just going to go to my room for a bit.'I can see the breakup is sinking in. 'I will cook another barbeque for dinner. Call you when it is ready.'

Skyla lies on her bed, and the realization is too much for her and sobs into her pillow.

Work

♥

Week 2

Skyla has opened up about her feelings she still has with her ex. She has stopped going into her room to sulk. I have made her laugh through the hurt and really listen. We have formed a friendship bond, and in return for giving her a shoulder to cry on, Skyla has been giving me tips on how to put myself first.We have been going out to coffee shops in the evening and a few cocktail bars to unwind from work. Skyla has been preparing me for this weekend by talking about her family and what they are like. She is preparing me for what to expect, so I do not feel unprepared.Skyla has been more in the room with me, and her thoughts have been in the present. She keeps telling me how she is so lucky to have met a nice guy like me. I have been enjoying her company myself and have talked more about what kind I woman I want to meet. Eventually, Skyla has opened up with to me about the guy she wants to end up being married to. She unexpectantly realized the person she wants to be with is nothing like Brad.

There have been many times she has not locked the door to the bathroom and accidentally walks in while she is having a shower or bath. Skyla has been laid back about it and she apologizes to me for not locking the door, when it should be me saying sorry. A couple of times I have seen her bum and breasts without her noticing and cover my eyes right away. One time I saw her full frontal nude when I was having a bath and she thought I was running it for her. She walked right in and dropped her robe to get in the bath and both shriek at the same time. She turns round to hide her modesty while exposing her bum and I submerge under water to hide from embarrassment.Each time, we can open up about it and find it amusing, like we are brother and sister. I think it has helped the both of us to feel comfortable around each other in such a brief space of time.

Skyla no longer comes home with a long face except for being exhausted. I now see her opening the door with happiness to see me and asks what plans are for tonight. I guess a heartache shared is a sadness halved. You would not think she broke up from a five-year relationship.It feels like we have known each other for years.Skyla feels she has been feeling more comfortable around Richard because of opening up to him about her breakup. Also, catching him in the nude by accident has also helped.Skyla has been having odd dreams with Richard popping into her mind. The dreams are about the two of them getting drunk or the two of them have a swim together. Nothing sexual, but she wonders why they are of Richard. Skyla found the first week a struggle to focus on work. As the second week progressed, she found her concentration improving. Skyla would hide in the restroom to sob, but she was coping now.

Apart from her friend Carla, no one at work knows about her private life. Her friend has kept her distance to allow Skyla to have some space for herself. She felt touched being asked to be her reference for her new apartment. Carla is going to see if she is ready to open up by using the reference as an excuse.

My work team has gained headway with going through the list of suppliers and eliminating the genuine companies.John wants to have a meeting with me to get an update about how close my company is to preventing the newspaper from going into liquidation.

I thought I would use this opportunity to know John a little more on a personal level. We have the informal meeting in his office. Jessica and Alina have provided me a brief report of our findings so far.

John is the third generation to run the company, and he is in his late seventies. He is Caucasian with fair skin, staying out of the sun with dark gray hair and wispy and clean shaven. His height is five foot eight and filled out.

His three-piece suit pin stripe with a bow tie.

He has been married for fifty years with two grown up kids in their thirties and has carved out their own career and so not interested in inheriting the business.

Before he took over the business from his dad, he gradu-ated in medicine and was to begin his career at Los Angeles Medical Center. But, his father suffered a stroke, and it forced him to give up his career to take over the business. His heart was not in it and allowed the board to run it.

John is behind his desk, and I sit in one chair in front of his desk. The meeting goes on for thirty minutes and we soon discuss each other's background. We move from his desk to his leather sofa.

I ask him about his plans for the future, 'Once we get your company on track, what will do? You must have plans to retire.'

John has been thinking about it a lot. 'I do not know. My kids have forged their own career and want nothing to do with the company. They have seen how much I have not been around. They have children of their own and they don't want to not see them grow up. They also saw how their grand dad became ill and they didn't want it to happen to me.'

I see how he has regrets. 'I notice that the company gives money to hospitals and I assume that is not a tax saving exercise. Is that your way of being near close to what is your dream job?'

John goes quiet as his mind goes back to his past. 'Yeah. You seem to know a bit about me.'

I smile and chuckle. 'Thats my job. To get to know my clients. Do you have regrets not following your dream?'

John's eyes say it all, 'Every day. But, I have my family and I would rather give up my career than my family. It has given me time to spend with my wife. If I became a doctor, I wouldn't be able to wake up one day and tell staff I am not going in today. Making time for my kids' birthdays. So, it is a double-edge sword. The business has given me freedom, but I would rather help save someone's life. Losing a couple of mills doesn't kill anyone. But being a surgeon is a difference between someone living or dying.'

I can relate to that, 'I think you made the right choice choosing your family and spending time with them over your career.'

John chuckles to himself, 'I guess you're right. How about you? Do you have a family?'

I am reminded again of being single, 'No. Never had the opportunity. Maybe it is because I spent my life in the office. And not letting my hair down and living life.'

John sees me with a sad face. 'Do you regret chasing the money instead of finding love and having kids?'

I have been thinking about it a lot recently, 'If I had known my life would be like it is today, I would have had a second thought putting work before life. I want a family and someone to go home to. But, I don't know where to start. Ask me how to save a billion dollar company, no problem. Ask me to find the one to love and grow old with. I do not know where to start.'

John tries to be helpful, 'I hear a lot about Tinder, eHarmony and Plenty of Fish around the office. How about starting there?'

I dread the thought of using dating websites, 'The thought of being overwhelmed by the number of women to review sounds like too much hard work. You know any?'

John has a suggestion, 'There is a girl in accounts. You have something in common already. She is about your age.'

I think I met her when we were shown around the office. 'I think I want to meet someone outside of accountancy.'

After we finish talking about life, I mention I am going to meet some investors tonight. John wonders if it is necessary, as he thinks the company has enough cash in the business and assets to leverage loans. I tell him we should avoid bank loans because of the current economy with risks of inflation causing the interest rates to rise. A hundred million is a lot if interest change by only a quarter of percent. That would be $250,000 in interest.

I explain private investors will not cost his company anywhere near that regarding returns on investment.

Eventually, I leave his office and join my coworkers to find out where the company is draining money.

They provide an office for us to conduct our work. I go through with my team what they have so far. The discussion is on the suppliers and expenses. We are to get answers on the value of assets, but it will only use them as an incentive for investors. So, it is not important for now.

I ask the girls to talk us through it.

Alina takes the lead. 'We went through all the company suppliers. We finally found one that does not exist. We check to see if they are registered as a corporate business. The company did not come up. We have looked into the transactions made to the supplier to see what expenses they record the costs. They come under the cost of sales. We saw it related them to material costs. Now, for a newspaper company, material costs will be the paper, delivery charge, ink and maintenance of the machines. So, we worked out the supplier costs related to paper. The transactions first started five years ago. At first, increments like a thousand dollars here and two thousand there. As the person got confident, it turned to hundred of thousands. They overlooked it as the size of cost was not material against the total cost of sales which runs in the million. Auditors are only interested in a figure that makes up over 10%. A $100,000 against a million is 10%.'

I know it is not enough to cause the company to go into disrepair, 'What else have you found?'

Jessica has something to say. 'That is not all we found. We looked into the miscellaneous account, and it opened a can of worms. That when we hit the jackpot. There are millions of dollar values recorded in the account. The auditors overlooked it because they didn't investigate the account. It would have caused them problems no end and risk having them sued for wrongly giving a going concern report.'

I know we need to delve into the ledger and pull it apart. 'I guess you are going to analyze the account and follow the money.'

Mark rolls his eyes. 'It is going to take a month to examine every transaction. We only planned to be here another two weeks.'

I already know, 'That is why I initially allocated a month. I think you can do it in three weeks. By that time, I will have the capital we need in place to bail them out.'

Therefore, I have these guys working for me. I tell them I will go to another office to make calls to the investors. I want to confirm dinner tonight. After I have confirmed the time and place, I will head back to the villa.

Skyla's day is going slow and her eyes are going blurry, staring at the computer screen. She is studying the Asian market and creating a report on the risk, trading in securities. It is going to take her all week to dissect. She has five ring binder folders opened up and overlapping each other, in front of her keyboard and monitor.

Carla walks over from her open plan office to see how she is going. 'I sent the form off for your reference, to do with the apartment. I thought I would come over and see how you are. It's been two weeks since I last saw you.'

Skyla is oblivious to the question as she fights with the folders. 'This is going to take a week to get through this. Thanks for sorting out the reference. Fancy having lunch together?'

Carla can see how stressed she is with work. 'Wanted to know how you are. Hows the current place? Have you been finding company?'

Skyla exaggerates an exhale of breath. 'My life is going from bad to worse. I had a call thirty minutes ago saying I cannot move in for another four weeks. Which means the second week of August. The villa won't be available until the end of July. I will have to find another place for two weeks. On top of that, my parents want to see me at a family party this Saturday. They don't know I have broken up with Brad. Luckily, they never met him. So, I am going to pretend we are still together. Richard is going to pretend to be my fiance.'Carla seems to have missed six seconds. 'Who is Richard? How did you meet him? Is he a potential boyfriend?'

Skyla is a matter of fact. 'Richard is someone who was renting the place for a month. My friend got his bookings mixed up. Thanks to Richard, he still let me stay. And I feel guilty because while I have been wallowing in self pity, he has done nothing but be kind and sweet. Making dinner every night, giving me space and checking on me. Thanks to him, he allowed me to unload everything and bounce off him. I would still be in a worse place if not for him.'Carla is keen to know more about him. 'What does Richard look like? Does he have a decent job? Is he single, married, got kids?'

Skyla takes an enormous sigh. 'Richard is single, has his own business, and is very rich. He is a gentleman with no baggage. But he is not my type. He is annoying with how he likes everything in its place. Richard plans before he speaks. He has a limousine for a car. But has offered to be my pretend fiance tomorrow.'

Carla wants to know more. 'How rich is he? Where does he live?'

Skyla playfully slaps her on her forearm. 'It is rude to talk about money. But he told me he is worth two hundred million.'

Carla's jaw drops. 'I would be happy to find him annoying for two hundred million dollars. Where does he live? Beverly Hills?'

Skyla waves her hand across her face. 'He lives in New York. But he rents a mansion here as an investment.'

Carla finds her funny. 'Why don't you marry him?'

Skyla finds other excuses. 'He is an accountant. Boring. And his teeth are too perfectly straight.'

Carla thinks she is falling for him. 'I think you are making excuses so not to have feelings for him. And calling the kettle black, you play with numbers too.'

Skyla screws up her face. 'Yes, but, but, my work is exciting.'

Carla does not care about that. 'He sounds perfect. I would swap him for my husband?'

Skyla gets up and walks over to the printer. 'And did I tell you he is rich? He bought a mansion just to rent it to film companies. He has a house he had built in New Jersey and has around two hundred million dollars.'

Carla's jaw drops again as she interrupts Skyla from taking the paper from the printer. 'Have you kissed? Slept with him? Made yourself get pregnant so you get allo mony?'

Skyla pretends to be disgusted by her thoughts. 'No. I don't know him that well. Not that I would. Not the pregnancy and allo mony. But I am struggling to get over Brad. He really hurt me. The last thing on my mind is to kiss another man not much sleep with him.'

Carla dares her. 'I'll give you fifty dollars if you sleep with him?'

Skyla changes the subject now. 'How about you come over and see for yourself?'

Carla would love to but doesn't feel comfortable. 'I'll give you a rain check. I have a busy married life. Do you have a picture of him?'

Skyla looks at her oddly. 'Why would I have a picture of him?'

Carla has to get back to work, but she is glad she came over to see if she is okay. 'See you at lunchtime.'

As Carla walks back to her desk, Skyla hears her phone ring. She wonders who could be calling her at work. She always tells her friends not to call at work.

I call Skyla to let her know I will be out for dinner tonight. I do not want her to worry about where I am. This morning I forgot to mention I have a meeting tonight. She will have to defend for herself tonight. I know she will be fine by herself as she has changed so much after talking to me about her problems.

Skyla picks up after a second call. 'Is everything okay?'

I put her at ease straight away. 'I forgot to tell you this morning that I have a dinner meeting tonight. I didn't want you worrying where I was. Not that I have to tell you my whereabouts.'

Skyla feels down in the dumps and is not sure why. 'Don't worry about it. I just thought I could cook for you tonight. For all the things you did for me. Meaning an ear to listen to my problems and a shoulder to cry on. It is my way of saying thanks.'

I sense she is sad to hear I am not in tonight. 'Well, we can do that tomorrow. Go out for something to eat. You can pay.'

Skyla does not know why she is jealous. 'Thats a deal. It's a shame it is not a social event. I feel kind of jealous someone else has your company tonight. Not that I'm saying I like you as like you. It's just I will kind of miss you tonight. It will feel strange you not being there tonight.'

I now want her to be there as I will pine for her company. 'Well, to be honest, they are going with their wives. So, I would feel the odd one out. If you would like to come out, you're more than welcome. You don't have to if you don't. I will leave it to you.'

Skyla does not need asking twice. 'I'll love to. What time?' I think out load, 'Dinner is at seven o'clock. I was going to go from here. But, I can pick you up around six thirty? At your office.'

Skyla sounds happy again. 'It's a date. I mean, it's a date to go out as friends.'

Business Dinner

♥

I leave the office with a spring in my step and do not know why. For the first time in my life, I have excitement about going out tonight. Having Skyla at the dinner makes me feel excited about going. I text Skyla when I leave in the limousine that I am on my way to her place of work now.

Skyla hears her cell phone ping, and she knows it is Richard. She smiles to herself and is quick to pack up. As she does, her boss turns up.

Her boss is curious about why she is going home early. 'You're leaving early. Thought you would be working hard to get the promotion.'

Skyla feels awkward about leaving early and lies. 'A friend has asked me to help him... I mean her out. She is going through a hard time.'

Her boss smiles at her, 'For someone who is going to the rescue of her friend, you seem thrilled about it. I saw you smiling as you peeked out of the window. And you said to him first. And from the looks of things, he is in that limousine. Does he have money and if so, get him to invest in our firm?'

Skyla goes quiet and bright red. 'I do not know what you are talking about. I was thinking of a joke someone told me earlier and it is my friend I can see waiting on the sidewalk.'

Her boss looks out of the window. 'What? That pin size person who I couldn't tell if she was my aunt. And there are few standing around.'

Skyla goes even more red. 'You got me. It is a guy. But, this is the first time in months I have finished before seven o'clock.'

Her boss laughs at her, 'Pulling your leg. Gotcha didn't I.'

Skyla nervously laughs. 'Right. I knew that. Ah ah ah. So, is it okay to leave?'

Her boss ponders for a minute, 'Is he your husband? I notice a ring on your finger.'

Skyla completely forgot she is still wearing her engagement ring. 'Huh. Yeah. Thats right.'

Her boss knows nothing about her personal life. 'He has never been to our retreats. Why not?'

Skyla feels really awkward. 'He has been busy every time.'

Her boss wants her to bring him along. 'I want to meet him. To see who puts a big smile on your face.'

Skyla wonders how she will get out of this. 'I can't promise he will make it. He is a very busy man.'

Her boss does not know a man who works at the weekend, 'Even on a Sunday? Do you even have time to make love?'

Skyla is not sure whether to use that as an additional reason for how busy he is. 'Yes. Even for that?'

Her boss' jaw drops. 'He is definitely coming. Or I will call him myself and have a go at him, neglecting you.'

Skyla has a knee jerk reaction. 'Yes, of course. I will guarantee he will be there. From Friday night through to Sunday.'

She now wonders how she will explain this to Richard as now he has to pretend to be a fiance and a husband now.

Carla can hear Skyla and their boss' conversation from across the office and is curious to what they are talking about.

Carla notices her leaving her desk and heading to the elevator. 'Hi Skyla. I am confused. You said you were miserable and still getting over the breakup. Is that a face of excitement?'

Skyla has no idea what she is talking about. 'I am sad. Now, I am depressed because our boss thinks I have a husband and wants to meet him. So, this is not an exciting face about going out with Richard. It is an exciting face getting away from the boss.'

Carla glees at her. 'I am so glad someone is making you happy.'

Skyla tries to convince her it is not Richard before the door closes. 'I am happy I am leaving. Not because I am seeing Richard.'

Carla taps on the closed elevator doors while she smiles to herself, seeing her friend smile again.

I check my watch, wondering why she has not come down yet. I am anxious about being late. As I worry, Skyla startles me when she opens the door.

Skyla is flustered. 'Sorry I kept you. My boss caught me at the wrong time.'

I already calm down when I see her face. 'No problem. What did he want?'

Skyla stutters, 'I'll tell you later. I don't want to think about work right now.'

I think no more of it. 'Hope you're hungry. We are going to a "La Boucherie", place my client suggested earlier in the week.'

Skyla has heard of it and shows a surprise face. 'I know it is a silly thing to say, but do you know how expensive that place is?'

I am more interested in getting the investors on my side. 'I will claim the bill for my business. Now, if they ask what we are, just tell them the truth. We are friends. I don't need you to pretend that we an anymore than friends.'

Skyla has such a glow about her. 'Thank you for inviting me. If I forget to say, I had a great time.'The manager welcomes us as we walk into the entrance of the restaurant. I give him my name and he instantly knows what table we are at.

The restaurant organises a round table in the corner where we can see the entire city. We are naturally the last to arrive. I watch her reaction to see if I impress her. See her glow makes this business dinner worthwhile.

I arranged for four of my closest business associates to have an opportunity of paying money in a failing company that is easy to turn around.

They are Fred, Brian, George and Simon. I have known them for years now through acquaintances.

Fred is Caucasian with dark brown hair and is in his forties. He is five foot eight with a slim build and wearing a brown evening suit. He is from Texas and likes to take risks with high returns.

His wife is called Devlin and they have three kids who are at college now and she is Caucasian and of a similar age.

Brian is also Caucasian, with blonde hair going slightly gray and in his late forties. He is five or six with a slight paunch, wearing a plain, light blue shirt with dark trousers and a beige blazer. He is from San Francisco near Silicon Valley and he enjoys investing in anything that has technology.

His wife is called Melissa and they have a couple of kids who have graduated already and in their respective careers. She is a couple of years young than him.

George is Asian with black hair and in his late thirties. He is five foot five with a very slim frame, wearing a black two-piece suit and a pale blue shirt. He is from New York and likes to dabble in pet projects. His primary interest is running his family clothing store chain.

His wife is called Vivian and they have no children yet and she is in her early thirties.

Simon is black with a bald head and is in his early fifties. His height is six feet tall with a wide frame, wearing a pair of jeans, a white shirt and a brown blazer. He owns an insurance company and has an interest in long-term investment. He is from Seattle.

His wife is called Monica, and they have three grown up kids doing their own things.

The eight of them all have eyes on us as we approach the table and take our seats.

Brian appears to be surprised. 'You never told us you got married.'

The others congratulate us, and I do not know how to come up to that conclusion. It is not like I gave them the impression or Skyla said something. I pretend I did not hear that.

Brian reaches his hand out. 'Let me see that ring. Wow, you didn't hold back buying that ring. When did you get married? When did you have a girlfriend?'

Monica stares at us. 'She is gorgeous. Where did you find her?'

Vivian cannot believe his bachelor days are over. 'How did you meet? You both look really suited together.'

Simon is annoyed that he did not know, 'Why didn't you invite us to the wedding? I thought we were friends.'

I stutter and lost for words, 'Um. Huh.'

Skyla jumps in. 'It is my fault. After we first met. It was a swirl wind, and he wanted to invite everyone, but I was too hasty. I found my man, and I didn't want to lose him to another girl. It was a shotgun wedding. Right, babe.'

I have no idea how to get out of it now and go with the flow, 'Like she said. This is Skyla. Skyla, this is George, Bruce, Simon and Fred. And their wives.'

The wives each introduce themselves to Skyla and eventually have our drinks ordered while we decide what to eat.

We do not talk about work, as Skyla and I are the focus of attention.

Simon is wants to know more, 'You have our money. So, need to discuss the details of the investment you want us to make. The last time we saw you, it was seven months ago. You were nowhere near having a girlfriend. What happened?'

I have to think on my feet, 'We were in Las Vegas at the time, weren't we? Well, on my way back to the holiday home I rented, I went to catch a taxi. And there she was, trying to get the same one. We were arguing over who got the taxi first and someone else ended up taking it. We ended up laughing and wondering why we were being so silly fighting over a taxi.'

Skyla sees me struggling and continues, 'Then I offer an olive branch by offering a drink. One drink lead to dinner and before we knew it, we ended up liking each other.'

Vivian goes cooey, 'You look so cute gazing into each other's eyes. What was it you found falling for him?'

We both struggle to decide who will answer first.

I see her getting flustered. 'It was her eyes. Her eyes. I suddenly realized how brown and dark they are. Before I knew it, I drowned inside them.'

Skyla realizes me going into deep thought and finds it awkward. 'And I fell for his smile. The moment I made him laugh, I knew I had him.'

We both lock eyes and forget they are in the restaurant with us. I have no idea why we are staring at each other when we have shown no interest in each other.

Simon snaps us out of it. 'I guess you are still in the honeymoon stage. Trust me, that will go,'

Monica playfully smacks him in the arm. 'Speak for yourself. Don't believe him.'

I play it down, 'And here we are. Like she said, we couldn't wait.'

Skyla says the same while clearing her throat, 'Likewise. And now we are here.'

Thinking that would be the last, Melissa asks about the honeymoon.

We are both lost for words and neither of us are not sure who to answer.

Melissa is on a baited hook. 'Well?'

I quickly jump in. 'Skyla loves the beach and seeing local markets. So, that's what we did.'

Skyla has a surprise face. 'Wow. And that is what happened.'

Vivian wants to know about more. 'Where did you go?'

Skyla goes off on a tangent. 'I always loved to go to Mexico. There is a love beach. There is this perfect spot I heard of called "Riviera Maya". It is, I mean, it was where I always wanted to go for a honeymoon or do as a couple. I wanted my last fiance to take me there.⫯

I notice her in deep thought and realize she is thinking of her exboyfriend. 'She means me. She always talks pretence. We were engaged. Duh, right Skyla.'

Skyla snaps out of a trance. 'Yes. Sorry. I was just reminiscing about our holiday. Wow, I'm starving. Is the waiter going to come back for our orders?'

During our meal, the conversation finally changes to the others, finding what they have been up since I last saw them. Before we know it, it is gone nine o'clock and we have only begun our desserts.

The night has gone better than I thought, apart from giving the wrong impression we are together and wondering why Skyla did not correct them. Also, I did not even notice she had an engagement ring on. The thing is big and I do not know why I missed it. I also wonder why she is still wearing it and why the guy did not ask for it back.

While thinking about how the evening is going, I accidentally dribble custard down the side of my mouth. I excuse myself in case anyone noticed and before I have time to grab my serviette, Skyla already reaches over and dabs my chin. She smiles at me as mops up the sauce and our eyes catch again.

Devlin goes cooey, 'How romantic and sweet. I wish Fred would be like that with me.'

Fred groans, 'I do. You just never notice.'

We all laugh at his comment and, for the first time in my life, I have a brief glimpse of what it is like to be in a relationship. Looking out for the other person.

Eventually the evening comes to a close, and the men put in our credit cards to cover the bill. I notice everyone cuddling each other except for Skyla and me. My knee jerk reaction is to quickly hug Skyla to keep up the pretence and not give it away that we are not a couple. Before I can hope she does not get offended, Skyla reciprocates and touches my hand.

It surprises me, and I think we make a great team fooling people.

After we say our goodbyes on the sidewalk, Skyla and I get into our limousine and head back to the villa.

I turn to Skyla and show my appreciation. 'Thank you for a nice evening. For the first time in my life, I didn't feel like the gooseberry and feel sorry for myself being single.'

Skyla gushes and shows her appreciation. 'For the first time since being dumped, I never once thought about Brad. So, thank you.'

I think about my extra stay here. 'It will feel weird when you are gone. I have to stay in LA for another four weeks. It is taking longer than I thought. You will already be in your apartment.'Skyla is surprised. 'Funny you should say that. I had a call today. I cannot move in until the second week of August. So, I'm glad you're still here as I have nowhere to go at the end of July.'We are both glad how things have turned out hanging out with each other for another four weeks.

When we get back to the villa, I fumble with the door key, trying to open it. When we walk inside, the atmosphere feels like it has changed. We both act differently round each other. Skyla is quick to say goodnight and head to her bedroom.

I am not ready for bed and so switch on the television and pour myself a glass of wine as a nightcap.

A romance film is on the channel and while watching it, I think about tonight and how refreshing it was not having the conversation of "when will I meet some?"

Skyla comes out of her room briefly to get something from the kitchen. 'I would stay up, but I am exhausted. Don't think I am trying to avoid you.'

I am shocked by her comment, 'No problem. I thought I had made you feel awkward or something.'

Skyla casually dismisses my assumption. 'I had a really nice evening. Thank you for inviting me. Goodnight Lewis.'

I say good night remembering her offering herself to come with me but I do not remind her of that conversation.

Apology

It is Saturday morning, and I have been wondering whether it was fate we are together for another four weeks. Not that I like her in that way, but I am enjoying her company. She is like a drug where the more I spend time with her, the more I want to be in her company. I guess I like her humor and how quirky she is.Skyla wakes up thinking about today with her family and hoping they do not spot Richard as a fake fiance. She is not worried about today. She is not sure why she is not nervous about introducing Richard as Brad.Her thoughts turn to how grateful she is with Richard staying for another four weeks. She would have been living on the streets. Also, she seems to be grateful to be spending more time with him. There is something about Richard she really likes about him, and she does not know what it is. To her, the more time she spends with him, the more she is going to hate saying goodbye.In the first week, all she could think about was not wanting to face the world. The pit of her stomach was aching from the loss of Brad. She did not want to be around Richard when she wanted to have a burst of tears. Now, coming up to the third week, she seems to skip a heartbeat if she thinks she will not see Richard all day. He is like a hit of expresso to her. Without her coffee, she will not function the rest of today. But she does not know why. It is not like she likes him in that way. She sees him as an older brother who will be there for her.The thought of Richard being there today comforts her.

I am the first to get up and, for the first time, going for a swim while I wait for Skyla to wake up and tell me what the plan for today is. During my swim, I have time to collect my thoughts and think of the future regarding wanting to meet someone and settle down with kids. Internet dating is not my thing and the thought of trying to type my interest and talk about myself from a marketing point of view does not sit with me. I also know that I have to change my working habit. All I have done is eat, sleep and drink in the office. My typical day is going to work at eight in the morning and finishing at eight in the evening. Only leaving me time to get home, wind down and be in bed by eleven. The weekend would meet up friends who are looking for the next big deal and new companies who are getting into financial trouble.

I think through how I will break the cycle and stick to it and each time I come up with an idea; it goes back to actually taking myself away from the office and the business as a sabbatical leave. Telling myself to let go, let Simon take over the reins and focus solely on my personal life and find a woman. Each time I think about that, I feel that life is about working and making money. When life is about living and spending it with love ones and enjoying other person's company. Work and money is a byproduct, not the direct importance.

Skyla eventually merges from her bedroom and comes outside to find me. I stop swimming and paddle towards the edge of the pool where she is. She seems up beat and thinks she is coping better with her breakup. I guess the long hours of talking about her feelings have helped her to move on. I know she is nowhere near being over him, as that would not be realistic. It has only been two weeks, and no gets over an ex that fast.While Skyla was pouring her heart out to me about Brad, I searched on the internet how long it can take to get over someone. I read it can take a minimum of eleven weeks to get over someone and up to eighteen months to heal from a marriage. Skyla has a long way to go before she can think about meeting someone new.

I stare up at her and she stares right back at me and eventually tells me she wants a chat. I climb out of the swimming pool, wrap a towel around me, and then take a seat at the table.

Skyla composes herself before opening up. 'I want to thank you formerly for helping me to unload all my baggage. You do not know how much you have helped me to let my feelings out. It is like an enormous weight has come off my shoulder. And, for agreeing to be my fiance for the day. Just glad I never gave back the engagement ring to Brad.'I was happy to listen to her. 'You don't need to thank me. If I didn't want to listen, I would have gone out every night. And I would have bought a diamond ring for the charade. So, no problem. You have given me a lot of insight into women.'Skyla cannot believe how kind he is. 'I hope the girl you meet really appreciates how great you are. If I was black, I would date you. Not that I like you in that way, but you are genuine and don't use your money or status to win people over.'

I joke with her, 'You can always sit under a tanning bed until you are totally black.'Skyla laughs at my humor, and eventually she causes me to laugh with her.After we finish making each other laugh, I ask what the plan is for today.Skyla knows I do not have any social clothes. 'First thing, we buy you new clothes. You can not show up in a thousand dollar suit.'I correct her, 'A two thousand dollar suit. But, carry on.'

Skyla cuts her eye at me. 'As I was saying, you need to wear informal clothes. I will take you shopping, come back here and then see my family. Because it is my problem, I will pay for your clothes. You have paid for everything else so far. It is only right I pay this time.'I have no problem with that.

Skyla knows where we should go for some suitable clothes, which is in 'Beverley Plaza'. There, Skyla takes the lead and wants to buy me a couple of polo tops, surf shorts, a pair of flip-flops, casual trousers and jeans.

Today, she wants me to wear a pair of jeans with a polo shirt. She is efficient, only taking an hour to find what she wants.

The party is at an outdoor event and it is her brother's birthday and he will be forty. Her parents organized the party at the Kenneth Hahn State Recreation Area. I have the limousine take us there, but Skyla wants us to park somewhere out of sight. She does not want to draw attention to herself being seen by her parents coming out of the car. I respect her and the driver has an idea where he can set us off.

The park is vast and has plenty of space for activities planned throughout the day. When we arrive, the driver stops in front of trees at the edge of the park. It is impossible for any of her family to see through the thick tree trunks. We then walk from there taking a few minutes.

When we appear in view, her family notice us straight away and would appear to be the last to arrive. I watch Skyla's reaction and see she was becoming anxious. I feel compelled to hold her hand and squeeze it to remind her I am here.

The first person to greet us is one of her sisters and hugs her.

Her sister pulls away and is keen to know who I am. 'Are you going to introduce us?'

Skyla gets flustered. 'Huh, this is Brad.'

Her sister appears impressed with her choice in man. 'I think I would keep him to myself as well. Where have you been hiding him?'

I now see what direction we are going and I play along. 'Skyla never told me how gorgeous her sisters are.'

Her sister is impressed with my response. 'Wow. You can come anytime. If I was not married with kids, my sister would have competition.'

I like her sister. 'I wouldn't let that stop you. But I don't think Skyla would allow me.'

Her sister laughs and shows her approval and leads us to the rest of her of family.

Skyla mouths to me, 'I'm so sorry. Thank you.'

I squeeze her hand and whisper in her ear, 'Don't forget to put the ring on.'

Family Pretense

♥

Her family has set up a table and chairs with picnic blankets. Everyone has brought food for everyone to eat. If I had known, I would have brought drinks at least.

The kids are running around nearby laughing and playing.

They swamped us when we approach her family, sitting and standing around making conversation. They stop what they are doing and make time to introduce themselves to me and to keep remembering the name Brad.

Skyla cannot believe how welcoming they are towards me and she becomes relax. They hug me and shake my hand like I have known them for years.

I can sense her siblings her siblings are openly talking about us among themselves. But all good and not malicious. Skyla's family is lovely and I can see why her personality is so warm.

I have to keep reminding myself that my name today is Brad.

Now and again, Skyla apologizes to me for not being honest with her family. For me, it doesn't matter as I will not be meeting them again after my six weeks here finishes. Skyla can think of a reason to why I am no longer around.

Eventually, I am introduced to her mum by Skyla and do not make a big thing of it. Her mum is happy to meet Brad, finally. She cannot believe no one has put a drink in our hands and takes us to the refreshments.

Skyla asks what is happening today. 'Are we going to sing happy birthday to my brother? Did you bring a birthday cake?'

Her mum tells us what is going to happen. 'We are going to play some games, have food and later on blow the candles.'

Skyla is conscious of the time. 'When are we going to finish for the day?'

Her mum is not worried about that, 'Whenever people are ready to go home. Brad, I hope you like baseball, one legged race, bowls and hit the pinata.'

This is going to be a long day, and I can see Skyla not wanting to be here longer than we have to be. But I reassure her it is going to be okay and tell her how much I like her family.

Skyla wonders off catching up with her siblings and her nieces and nephews while I find a seat and have a cold bottle of water. I observe her family and in laws and realize they married into other cultures. Her siblings have married a Mexican, a black guy and an Asian. There are extended families invited, which I only noticed.

This reminds me of my family when there is a get together and wonder how they would react if I brought a white girlfriend home. All my siblings married a black person and, like Skyla, have a few nieces and nephews. Today is really hitting home with how much I want to start a family.

As I mull over my thoughts, her sister comes over who I first spoke to and sits next to me. I am not sure whether to begin the conversation or wait for her.

Her sister makes the first move. 'So, what do you think of the mad family? Is it what you expected?'

I look at her family interacting again before I answer. 'I like it. There is a real mixture of ethnicity. I would not have thought so looking at Skyla. She has never talked about how diverse your family is. Sorry, I didn't get your name.'

Her sister laughs, 'Paula. They are a crazy bunch. We argue like any other family, but that is how we roll. Do you have a big family, Richard?'

I compare the two. 'Much the same. But my family has not mixed with other cultures. But, my family grew up in the Bronx. There are few other nationalities in the Bronx.'

Paula is worldly, 'Huh, yes. You have the "Apollo Theater", Bill Clinton has an office there and the only black bank there. I totally get it. If, where we live was not multicultural, we would be stuck one of the two cultures.'

I lean away from being in shock. 'You seem to know a lot. Where does that come from?'

Paul cuts her eye. 'My parents are working class, and they had nothing. They made friends with anyone and everyone. They became teachers, and they had to start somewhere.'

I see now where she gets her knowledge, 'Don't tell me, you parent's worked in the Bronx. Back then, there were no black teachers.'

Paul claps her hand. 'Now you're getting there. So, what about your parents?'

I briefly describe them, 'Like your parents, working class. Dad worked in the postal service and mum worked as a nurse. They are no longer working now. I...my siblings and I now financial support them. They don't have to work ever again.'

Paul is doting on me. 'You are winning me over even more. Your siblings help with their living and medical bills?'

I try not to be proud, 'We pay for a full-time nurse to take care of them in their house. We have done well for ourselves and so we bought them a house in a friendly area to spend out the remaining days.'

Paul is speechless. 'Skyla has found a catch. Your siblings must be well off.'

I half laugh. 'Something like that. Like your family, we worked hard. Nothing was given to us.'

Paula is called over to help with unpacking the food. 'It is nice talking to you. Speak to you later.'

I catch Skyla glancing over at me, and I guess she saw us talking. She smiles at me with joy in her eyes and sees that she is no longer scared or nervous. I walk over to her to find out what was said.

Skyla is laughing at the kids running around and the adults acting silly and being affectionate to one another.

I notice how her original thought of being interrogated has melted away. 'So, it is not as bad as you thought.'

Skyla bows her head in agreement. 'What did Paula have to say?'

I give her a summary, 'She wanted to know about my family and how I find yours. No question about how we met or how much I like you. How about you?'

Skyla gives me the same similar answer. 'They like you. They think you are a great catch. No questions about what your favorite color is. Which is what I was more worried about.'

I guessed they would just be happy to catch up with her. 'I thought they would not ask too many questions. And you were panicking over nothing. I can see they want to know you are happy. They only want you to be happy. Not if you are dating or close to being married. And, I like your family. They are really nice. They remind me of mine.'

Skyla continues observing her family interactions. 'Thank you.'

I wonder what will happen when I am gone. 'What will you do when I finish here and head back?'

Skyla hesitates to give me an answer. 'Not sure. Cross that bridge when I cross it.'

Skyla's mum calls for our attention to get involved in base-ball and we will be on the same team. There will be a team of five and we are with her in laws from her brother's side. They are the parents and one of his children. We are playing against her sister Paula and her in law with one of her children. Our team are going to field first and agree to have the mother-in-law throw and three of us try to catch them out. I take the lead and tell the father-in-law to stay on third base to tap them out.

Skyla covers the left side of the batters, and I cover the other side. The ball is a sponge and so we cannot hit it too far for us not to chase after the ball.

The mother-in-law throws the ball as best as she can with a dainty under arm toss. The batter is Skyla's brother. He hits the ball, and it runs along the ground. I dive for it and use my body to stop it from traveling any further. The rest of the family is cheering on her brother to move. I grapple with the ball and throw it towards the father-in-law. He catches the ball fumbling with it but her brother makes it on the third base. Skyla is very competitive and shouts at us to be more vigilant.

The next two batters can only make it on the first two bases. The last person to bat is the child. After hitting the ball, Skyla catches out her nephew and then runs after the two in laws and tag them out. She does not hold any prisoners.

It is now our go and Skyla and I think it is best to let the elders go first and her niece before us. I go last and when it is my go, Skyla is on first base and the in-laws and niece make it pass third base. After I hit the ball, I shout at Skyla to run, and the opposition has thrown the ball to Skyla's brother manning third base. As he goes to catch the ball, Skyla and I make it to third base and we fall over each other in the dry dusty dirt and avoid being tagged out. Skyla ends up on top of me as we laugh out loud, winning the game.

Skyla cannot help laughing in fits of giggles as she straddles Richard with her hands on either side of his shoulders. Her hair is blocking the view of his face and pulls her hair back. Something makes her stop laughing and stare at him. Her eyes

wonder to his mouth, nose, cheeks and eventually his eyes.
It is like she is in a trance.I see Skyla has stopped laughing,
which makes me stop giggling, and I study her face. I like the
shape of her mouth and how her cheeks have definition. The
best part I like about her face is her cute nose and are her ey
es.There is something strange as we do not say anything, and
it feels like the world has stopped. Eventually, Skyla moves
her head towards me and I feel compelled to move towards
her.Neither of us smiles at each other as we show no expre
ssion.Suddenly the world moves again and her family shouts,
"Get a room already!" They also jeer at us, which snaps us out
of our daze. Skyla goes all embarrassed and hastens off from
me. I feel awkward and silly and quickly adjust myself.The
kids act out being sick seeing two grown-ups going to kiss.We
struggle to make eye contact and can see her going bright red.
That is one advantage, being black.

After all the baseball games are finished, everyone sits down
for BBQ food and snacks supplied by various members of
the family. Skyla and I are put together at the table with her
parents.

Skyla's mum wants to know all about me as Brad, and wonders why Skyla has never introduced me to the family.

Skyla's mum wants to know more about our relationship.
'How long have you two been together?'

Skyla clears her throat. 'The past couple of weeks. Only
joking. Five years.'

Skyla's mum cannot believe it has taken all this time. 'It took
you till now to introduce him to us. What do you do for work,
Brad?'

I nudge Skyla under the table to stop her from answering. 'I
help companies who are struggling financially to prevent them
from going into liquidation. I also analyze transactions to see
if employees are stealing from the company or the board of

directors are shortening the stock value of the company, so cheap to buy.'

Skyla's mum's jaw drops after hearing about my job, 'Do you think he will do my tax? The IRS are crawling all over my...'

Skyla stops her there, 'Mum. Please. You have only just met him.'

Mum cannot stop asking questions, 'So, how did you meet?'

Skyla scratches her neck and getting flustered. 'It was at a house...house party. I thought he was gate crashing. Turned out I was wrong. He offered me dinner. Went from there.'

Skyla's mum has a surprise face how well he has settled in with the family. 'It feels like he has been a part of the family for years. Don't lose this one. I can see you two getting married and having kids.'

Skyla appears uncomfortable. 'I think Brad has heard enough. You're making me embarrassed.'

I am speechless, considering we have only known each other for two weeks. 'No one has ever said I am marriage material. That means a lot.'

Skyla realizes what she just said. 'I mean. I wish I met him years ago. He is a great cash. Did I tell you he is rich? I mean million rich.'

Mum laughs, thinking she is meaning proverbially, 'Funny. But I know what you mean.'

It is close to six o'clock and we both feel tired and ready to head back. Before we let her relatives know we are going, Skyla feels she should apologize for her mum. We have gone for a stroll to be by ourselves to talk. There is a nice walk path that overlooks the whole park.

I stop her there. 'You have nothing to say sorry for. They assume I am your fiance and so your mum is behaving that way. And clearly you were panicking and felt the need to avoid embarrassing questions to being single.'

Skyla cannot believe how chilled out I am about it. 'The woman you end up marrying will be so lucky to have you.'

I reassure her I am fine about it. 'This experience has given me the confidence to know that I am marriage material. And A family who has known me for only five minutes thinks I am good enough for their daughter. Not that I am giving you ideas or making you think I like you that way.'

Skyla feels relieved and we head back to the party to say our goodbyes.

After we spend twenty minutes saying good with her family, being glad to meet me and vice versa, eventually head off.

In the car, Skyla falls asleep and uses my shoulder as a pillow, and I find her breathing soothing. During our twenty-five minute drive, it allows me to reflect on today finding out what it will be like hanging out with someones in law. If I can get through that, I can handle any family in law.

Another part of today that struck a chord was when we almost kissed and I know I was not imagining it. She looked at me differently before compared to previous times.

When we arrive back at the villa, I assume Skyla will go straight to bed even though it is Saturday night and no work tomorrow. But she wants to relax in the living room before going to bed.

I make us hot chocolate to watch mundane television as background noise. Skyla takes her mug and asks me to sit next to her.

Skyla surprises me by asking how work is, 'Are you on track with salvaging the company?'

I think about how much progress they have achieved. 'The investors have already implemented their money into making an overall on their software and manufacturing machines. Three quarters of the way through unraveling the account. We believe there is someone cooking the books illegally. We are still trying for the end of the month but most likely second week of the April.'

Skyla sounds interested. 'What if you don't find the person? Will all your effort to turn the company round be wasted?'

I have never not completed a job, 'I have never failed. But if we don't find the person, then all our effort will be set back within six months.'

Skyla has this serious look I have never seen before. 'How easy will it be to flush them out?'

I am relying on my team to find the source, 'If my employees find nothing in two weeks, I will have to get my hands dirty. I used to reconcile accounts in my early career.'

Skyla holds my hand. 'I have faith in you and your people. And thank you for the best day with my family.'

She turns to face me and kisses me on the side of my cheek and then relaxes against me while we continue watching television.

Birthday Girl

♥

Week 3

Skyla has not stopped thanking me enough for being at her family party. I insist it was not a problem and enjoyed meeting her family.We avoid acknowledging the awkwardness during the baseball game when we tumbled together. It has not affected how we get along or friendship.We bounce off each other with making each other laugh.

It is Friday morning and we are both dressed and having breakfast together. I notice Skyla is a bit withdrawn and not sure if she is relapsing and going into a depression. It is only natural for people who go through a break up to go two steps forward and one step back.I make conversation to bring back her smile. 'What do you have on at work today?'Skyla is staring into space and snaps out of it. 'Oh, sorry. I have a couple of reports to hand over to the traders. How is work going for you?'I leave out the boring details, 'We found the employee who falsified a supplier to cypher money out of the company. And the funds are available to upgrade all the old machineries and implement new software licence. This will take the remaining weeks here. Have you got a lot on? You seem sad today.'Skyla opens up. 'It is my birthday today. It reminds me I do not have someone to share it with. Normally I would go out for dinner and then a movie.'

I feel for her and want to do something, 'We can go out for drinks, a meal or a movie. I will be back early. We take the limousine anywhere you want in the city.'

Skyla cheers up. 'I would like that. Can you pick me up from work and go straight out?'

I think I can do that, 'Yep. I will come for six o'clock and pick a restaurant with a cocktail menu. We don't have to work tomorrow, so we can lie in tomorrow.'

Skyla agrees to it. 'Great. I better get going. See you at six o'clock. Looking forward to it.'

Along the way to the client's office, I ask the driver to stop at a cake shop to buy a birthday cake. I leave it in the trunk to keep it out of the sun and also in a cool place.

My client wants to take me out to lunch today to have a mini celebration to reach a turning point.

John drives us to a restaurant in his Rolls Royce, which is his favorite place to eat. He asks me how things are going with Skyla as if we are dating. I had not realized how much I have mentioned her since providing work for him. I make it clear we only met three weeks ago, and she has split up from a long relationship. Also, I have no interest in her even though she is great for company and she is seriously attractive.

John appears to know the staff very well as they speak on first names. They have given us a different menu than their usual. They took us to a table for two and bring us water and bread while we choose from the menu.

John is overwhelmingly grateful, 'You are good at your job.'

I brush it off. 'It's my job. It's why you pay the big bucks. Let me pour that for you.'

I like the restaurant he picked, 'Spago' is a good choice. How did you get us here when you need reservation?'

John is humble, 'I made friends with the owner. I told him you are going to drag the family business into the 21st century. Improve the editing software.'

I have a thought of what to do for Skyla's birthday this weekend. 'I may ask the owner if I can take Skyla here for her birthday.'

John is interested in my dilemma. 'Does Skyla know you like her?.'

I play it down. 'What are you talking about?'

John can read me, 'She obviously means something if it bothers you about where to take her for her birthday.'

I put my elbow on the table and club my hands together. 'She broke up with someone three weeks ago, after five years. It had a profound effect on her, for obvious reasons. I want her to have a nice birthday so she doesn't think of her ex, Brad.'

John has a bizarre idea. 'I have a holiday home in Mexico. It was more of an investment than actually using it as a second home. Why don't you impress her by going there for the weekend?'

I briefly chuckle to myself. 'I remember her telling me last week that she always wanted to go to a place I have never heard of. Something, Mayo, May. I don't know.'

John seems to know exactly what she was talking about, 'Riviera Maya'. That's where my home is.'

I laugh to myself, 'You're kidding. What are the chances of that? You're kidding me, right?'

John chuckles, trying to be serious. 'I'm not joking. I bought a place out there because of it. It is everyone's choice of destination. It is not a secret.'

I am shocked, 'Maybe I will book a hotel there. Even though it maybe extravagant for a birthday.'

John insists I use his place to stay. 'I will give you my key to you before you go home tonight. I have a private plane you can borrow. For what you have done my business, it is the least I can do. Settled.'

I feel undeserving, 'You don't have to do that. I will think of finding somewhere to stay there.'

John is more insistent, 'Done. I will get my secretary to give it to you. I will call her now so I don't forget.'

I embarrassingly accept, 'Thank you. I will use my private jet. You have done enough. I just hope she will like it and not feel over the top.'

John smiles, 'She'll love it. She might even ask you to marry her afterwards.'

I find him humorous. 'I don't think so. We are completely different. We want different things.'

Our lunch arrives and we say no more about it.

Skyla has gone for lunch with her friend Carla, and they eat a sandwich from a deli van and take a seat on a bench opposite. They have a brief moan about how busy work is and rumors of a fling between two co-workers in accounts and sales. They laugh about the thought of them two being together. Eventually, the conversation turns to Skyla and Richard.

Carla thinks there is something going on between her and Richard. 'I notice you have barely sulked over, Brad. Does this mean you are getting over him?'

Skyla goes quiet, reflecting on what she said. 'I'm still hurting. It has only been three weeks.'

Carla can see she is healing. 'I think Richard is making you smile.'

Skyla tries not to laugh at her silly comment. 'We are just enjoying each other company. He goes back to New York in four weeks' time.'

Carla thinks he is staying for her. 'Don't you find it strange that he stays for a further two weeks when you're moving in date into your apartment is being delayed by two weeks?'

Skyla reads nothing into it. 'If he was into me, not that I would react to his advances, don't you think he would have come on to me by now?'

Carla sees it as a long game. 'He is waiting for you to be totally over, Brad. Then when you least expect it, pounce on you.'

Skyla laughs with her thinking she is being childish, ⍰ Carla remembers it is her birthday today. 'What you doing for your birthday today?'

Skyla tells her about tonight. 'Richard is going to take me out tonight. For dinner and cocktails.'

Carla has a surprised expression, 'Wow. Impressive. And you are still friends?'

Skyla is short with her. 'Nothing is going on. It has only been three weeks. I'm still getting over Brad. It is going to take at least six months to get over him.'

Carla feels guilty. 'I just want you to be happy. Since you've been living with him, you wouldn't think you broke up with someone three weeks ago. Whenever I mention his name, your eyes light up.'

Skyla does not believe her. 'No, I don't. Besides, I don't date millionaires.'

Carla can see her eyes say differently, 'Okay. Change the subject.'Soon after, they head back to work.

When I pick Skyla up, she is excited to leave work and let her hair down. I tell her about my new plan.I explain there is a new itinerary. 'We are going to go back to the villa first. We need to sort out a few things. Then we are going to spend your birthday in a completely different place. You'll love where we are going. But I am going to keep it a secret.'

Skyla is smiling from ear to ear. 'Are you going to give me a clue?'

I want to surprise her, 'No. But we will go on a plane.'Skyla holds my hand and squeezes with excitement.

Once we get to the villa, we go to our respective bedrooms and begin packing. I tell her to. Skyla occasionally shouts through the wall, asking if she should pack summer clothes, bikini and sun screen. I say to yes to all her questions, which gives her an idea what type of birthday surprise it will be.We both pack frenzily as I want to be in Mexico in the early hours.By seven o'clock, we are out of the front door and back in the limousine. I ask the driver to take us to the airport where my company jet is. Skyla never knew I owned a jet and her face shows shock. I think if I took her to the bottom of the ocean, I would still impress her as we were flying there on my jet.

Once we reach the airport, the air steward takes our travel suitcases, and I see Skyla is enjoying what it is like to be on the other side.

We were in such a hurry; we are still wearing our work clothes. I suggest we change into casual clothes during the flight. Skyla does not enjoy changing into fresh clothes without a shower. So, it blew her mind when I say there was a shower on the plane.

During the flight, we both have individual showers and change into our summer clothes. Skyla has changed into a pair of trouser shorts and a short sleeve blouse. I change into trouser shorts as well with a V neck T-shirt.Skyla's eyes wonder around the plane, fiddling with the switches to see what they do. She is like a kid in a candy shop.

Skyla brings up her ex fiance. 'Brad never organized a surprise this big.'

I assume he is not as rich as me. 'Not being funny, but is he a millionaire?'

Skyla smiles, 'No. You know what I mean. He never made a special effort for my birthday, like you have.'

I could do with some fun in my life. 'Well, you have been teaching me how to let my hair down.'

Skyla almost laughs. 'You don't have any hair.'

I glance up. 'I wonder why there was a draft. But, seriously, you have got me thinking about prioritizing my personal life. All I have done is work. When I get back to New York, I will think about making a change.'

Skyla is sceptical, 'You would give up this lifestyle?'

I think I am ready. 'I can't do both. I have devoted my time for too long to making money. No wonder I have never been seen.'

Skyla gives me advice. 'Just be yourself. And I promise someone will see you.'

I think is it easier to believe than accept, 'I worry that even if I put my work life on hold and focus on me, I still won't meet anyone. But, I want to know I did the best I could to find someone. I am ready for marriage and kids now. '

Skyla does not know how to prove me wrong. 'Well, when you meet your woman, call me.'

We have another four hours to reach 'Riviera Maya' in Mexico with an ETA of one o'clock in the morning.

When we reach Mexico, Skyla has an inkling of where we are, but not totally sure. We order a taxi as soon as we get our bags from the plane. I have the address from John and is only a fifteen minute drive from the airport.

Once we arrive at the villa, we both agree to go to bed now and wake up first thing in the morning to begin her birthday drinks.

The next morning, it is a beautiful sunrise with clear skies and the sound of the ocean drifting on the beach. I go to make coffee while Skyla is still in her bedroom, with no sign of movement.

I have already showered and put on new clothes from the shopping we did before her family party. Wearing a pair of surfer shorts and a V neck shirt. My plans are to take Skyla to the beach for the day and then go for drinks in the evening and repeat on Sunday before we get our flight back.

As I go to walk out into the outside decking area to drink at the garden table, Skyla surfaces and goes into the kitchen.

Skyla walks in a T-shirt that barely covers her bum in a thong. 'Have you left enough for another coffee?'

I almost drop my jaw when I notice her attire. 'Yeah. Have you noticed where we are?'

Skyla holds her coffee against her mouth. 'Riviera Maya?'

I can see her smile behind the coffee mug. 'Maybe.'

Skyla struggles to hold her gratefulness. 'Wow. Wow. And you have a problem getting a girlfriend. Do you know how much this means to me?'

I know but I play it down, 'I remember what you said at the business dinner. I found out my client owns a villa here and was here.'

After our coffee, Skyla showers and changes into a yellow two-piece bikini thong.. I cannot stop myself from staring at her very nice bum.

Skyla sees Richard with a fresh pair of eyes and she finds herself no longer having her mind scattered with Brad. She cannot stop observing his bum through his surfer shorts. Skyla finds his very few tight curls on his chest cute and his torso appealing to the eyes. She has never noticed how strong his legs are with big calf muscles.

She thinks it is relating to spending three weeks twenty four seven with him. It has crept up with her without realizing. She wonders what he would be like to sleep with and if he would know how to push her button.

Skyla asks me to put sun cream on her back and it feels awkward as I picture us making love and the view of her bottom does not make it easier to stop my imagination.

I ask her, 'Where do you want me to put the stuff?'

Skyla lays there on her front with her bikini top untied, 'All over my back. And can you put it on my bum cheeks?'

I turn away while dabbing her cheeks with the cream. Eventually massaging it in on her says so.

We stay on the beach for a few hours until close to three o'clock. Then we freshen ourselves up for an early night out for a four o'clock start.

Skyla goes to use the shower and accidentally walks in on Richard taking a shower, but he is oblivious to her presence. She sees a glimpse of his private and wishes she could undo what she saw. She does not regret accidentally seeing his naked body yet again.

Once we are ready, I call us a taxi and we head to the social scene near Xelha.

When we arrive, we pick 'Coco Bongo' to drink, at which is a nightclub. It is a random place we think of going to. I wear a pair of casual shorts with an untucked short-sleeve shirt. Skyla wears a loose blouse with a pair of casual skinny shorts which finish below her crotch. I do not know how she gained bronze legs after only a day.

I buy drinks for the evening, which only includes shots and no beer, wine or champagne. However, we take our time and pace ourselves every half an hour.

Our conversation is talking about the men and women in the nightclub and daring each other to go up to one of them for a quick kiss. But, we are all talk and have no guts. The more drinks we have, the more we talk about the women in next to no skirts and the men trying to show off their chests with gold medallion.

We have a tall table to stand round and prop ourselves up on. We finish our eight drinks and Skyla offers to use my card to pay for the next rounds. While I wait for her to come back, I do not notice a couple of women come up to me.

They are slim and wearing hugging fitting dresses who are not my type. I do not have the nerve to tell them to go away. This is Skyla weekend and not a weekend of one-night stands with a bunch of strangers.

They dance around me, twerking against me. I feel embarrassed and sorry for them as I will find the courage to reject them.

Skyla pays for the drinks and turns round to walk back to Richard. Her blurry eyes just make out two girls flirting with Richard. Her eyes soon sober up when sees the two women cavorting with him. She does not know what comes over her when she sees red. Whether it is the alcohol or caring about his wellbeing, she rushes over, almost spilling the drinks.

As I am about to find the polite words to tell them to go away, Skyla comes out of nowhere and bosses them about. I am shocked as I have never seen this side of her before. It is like I am her property and no one else can have me.

I freeze, not knowing how to handle the situation. Skyla asks the two girls to leave us alone. They ignore her request and I suggest we move to another table. Skyla begrudgingly agrees, and we walk away from them.Girl one tries to get a reaction. 'Are you afraid to lose you, man?'Skyla takes offence. 'He is not my boyfriend. But he can do better than you.'

I feel awkward. 'It's okay, Skyla. We'll leave.'Girl two takes an interest in me. 'Let me give you my number. If she can't do it for you, call me.'Skyla's eyes change. 'He is not interested in you.'

Girl one squares up to Skyla and the girl towers over her. I put my arm around Skyla's waist to push her away. As I do, Skyla stands her ground, and I do not see the girl punch Skyla in the face. She hits Skyla so hard; I fall to the ground with her.The two girls leave abruptly when a bouncer runs over.

Skyla is completely unconscious and my thought is to take her home in a taxi and take care of her.

I lift her limp body in my arms and carry her outside and go to the taxi parked outside. During the journey, I keep her in my arms and gently brush her hair away from her face. I see the girl in the bar gave her a nosebleed and a bruise on her cheek.

I See You

♥

The taxi driver asks if I want to go to the hospital, but I insist on taking us back to the house.Skyla is still unconscious when we get back to the house. I decide to carry her to the sofa and notice she has been bleeding heavily from a nosebleed. Her cheek is quite red and turning blue. I go into the kitchen to get a kitchen towel and ice from the freezer. Also, a bowl of water and a clean cloth.

Skyla is so pretty, lying there asleep and oblivious with dry blood from her nose bleed over her lips and chin. I apply the ice wrapped in towel to her cheek and she instantly stirs round from the pain. Her deep brown eyes adjust and refocus on me.

Skyla stares at me with concentration. 'What happened?'

I explain, 'You were being a lady. Trying to save me from two undesirable women. One of them punched you. I think you are going to have a shiner.'

Skyla is amusing. 'How did the girl fare?'

I tell her to be quiet, 'Shh. Let me clean your nosebleed. You scared me. I thought something more serious was going to happen.'

Skyla feels guilty. 'I'm sorry. At first, I didn't know why I was behaving like that. I suddenly realize something.'I have a blank mind. 'You're gay? You fancied the woman who punched you?'

Skyla tries not to laugh. 'Please don't make me laugh. It hurts.'I gently dab the blood away from her nose and mouth. 'This look suits you. Get married with this look.'

Skyla stops smiling and shows a serious expression. 'I see you.'I think she is delirious. 'Yeah, and I can see you. How many fingers?'

Skyla stares right into my eyes. 'No. I see you.'I think I know what she means and I get nervous. 'Don't joke with me. I don't need you to feel sorry for me.'

Skyla puts her finger to my mouth. 'Shh. I see you. I see you.'

I think how much I want to kiss her, 'Okay. I saw you the day I met you.'

I linger over her, thinking of her painful face. I ever so gently kiss her on the mouth. Even though it must hurt like hell, she kisses me back.

I carry Skyla to her bedroom and I help her change out of her clothes. As I do, Skyla wants me to do something which I have never done before. She wants me to pleasure her. I do not know where to begin, but she guides me.

Skyla is left with only her underwear and bra. 'Don't be shy. You have already seen me naked with the amount of times we walked into each other by mistake.'I stand at the foot of the bed and lean over her with my hands on either side of her body. She motions me to slide her under off. Skyla does not flinch as I reveal her vulva. I place her underwear next to her and slowly sly between her legs. She makes it easy for me to access her by widening her legs.Even though I have never done this before, I use my time spent watching raunchy internet sites. I copy actions from scenes I have watched before. I make eye contact with Skyla and read her emotions. Each time I touch her in the right place, she closes her eyes to magnify the sensation. I cannot help breathing in her musky scent as I slowly slide my tongue along the length of her folds before focusing on her button. It feels like a marble as I suck, lick, and rub.

Skyla quietly groans to herself and begins gently to gyrate her vulva against my mouth and feel her lactating. To push her over the edge, I slide my forefinger inside and inside and build up a rhythm. I can sense Skyla coming close to exploding as she speeds up, rotating her hips. I slide in a second finger and it is enough to bring her to ecstasy.As her body stiffens and her legs turn to jelly, I ride her vulva to extend her climax. I really enjoy hearing her vocals, knowing it is me who is satisfying her.

Skyla feels a sharp pleasant heat, and it begins with baby waves going through her body. As Richard learns her body language with each moan and groan, he pushes Skyla's button in the right places.

Waves of pleasure grow bigger until they are like tidal waves, which then sparks the best sensation she has ever had from a man. Her body stiffens and Richard keeps the pace to ride her ecstasy. Her feet point forward, almost flat as she is ready for her vulva to explode. Richard has to pin her hips down to continue stimulating her button.

Once the waves of her climax subside, I gently lick her vulva to watch her twitch and beg for me to leave it alone.I lie alongside of Skyla and stare at her, recovering from being pleasured.Skyla lays flat on her back and turns her head to me. 'I would have been happy with the feel of you on me. But that was ridiculous. I have never experienced an orgasm like that before. And you are single.'I smile and try not to laugh. 'I took some lessons. It helps when you are enjoying giving it. God, you are so beautiful.'Skyla moves in and kisses me, which turns into a passionate kiss. We enjoy each other's company until we fall asleep.

The next day, I sit outside on the decking and wait for her to wake up and provide company. Not sure how to behave around her. There was no formal agreement of how we move forward. We were both knew what we were doing to not call it a drunken session. We have three more weeks together and so we cannot pretend it did not happen.

Eventually, Skyla shows her presence a little after ten o'clock in the morning and appears awkward and not sure about approaching me.

Skyla is wearing another bikini in pink and has an orange color smoothie in her hand. She sits next to me and puts her feet on another chair. I have a feeling she wants to broach the subject, and I call the elephant in the room.

I choose my words carefully, 'I enjoyed last night. I know you are still coping with moving on from Brad. If last night was a one off, that is fine. I get it. We both lost our inhibition through drinking. I want to know if it was a one off because we have to live with each other over the next three weeks.'

Skyla takes her time, gathering her thoughts. 'I meant want I said last night. I find you attractive. But I know it will not amount to anything. Three reasons. You go back to New York in three weeks. Your preferred relationship is with a black woman. And I am not ready for another relationship. But, I realize I want a non commitment intimacy. If that is not your thing, I will have to live without it until I move into my apartment.

I won't take offense if you do not want to do it again.'I really liked last night. 'Even though I want to be with a black woman long term, there is no chance of meeting a black woman right this minute. I won't be looking until I get back to New York. I will not play games or make you second guess me. We did something last night that I really liked. Not sure about you, but I had a great time.'

Skyla smiles as she is relieved. 'Really? You're not just saying that?'

I reiterate, 'Trust me. If it was bad, I would say I don't want to continue doing it. Even though you did nothing to me, I found I got really turned on because you were getting aroused.'

Skyla covers her face and goes red. 'I cannot believe you said you have never done that before. I thought you were a professional. Somehow, you knew exactly where to find my hot spots. I thought I was going to have a heart attack.'

I move in the chair to lean towards her and whisper, 'I saw a lot of lesbian videos.'

Skyla laughs, and our eyes fix on each other once again. We stop laughing and begin kissing each other again. We agree to spend the morning together and go out this afternoon to the market.

We continue kissing inside the house in privacy. Skyla tugs at my shorts to take them off. As we fight to push our lips together, I can't get enough of her lips and mouth. I want to pleasure her again and give her the same experience as last night. I enjoy turning her on.My shorts and underwear are around my ankle now and it is not long before I feel my phallus getting hard. Skyla squeezes and pulls on my member while we continue to kiss passionately.Skyla whispers to me in-between deep breaths, 'I want to make you cum. I want to turn you on.'

I laugh at the notion she wants to pleasure me, so it is not one sided. I murmur to her I want that. Skyla pulls away and slowly goes down on her knees. She stares at my manhood as she plays with it in her palm.

Skyla, has a full concentration of my phallus and occasionally, glances at me as she wonders at the size of it.Eventually, she licks the end of my shaft, swirling and flickering her tongue. It is great feeling the texture of her tongue. Skylas tongue feels like a pear, grainy and soft. When she takes me inside her mouth, I find her sexy, with her head gently bobbing up and down and her ponytail swaying at the same time. I love the way how she takes her time and there is no hurry. Her eyes are closed and it is like she is in a trance.There has not been one woman who has shown me what pleasures me. Yet Skyla

knows without reading my signals.When Skyla comes up for
air, she rubs the end of my phallus with her palm while her
eyes are fixed on mine. She cannot help herself smiling at me
in the corner of her mouth.She has been working my member
for almost half an hour now, but she is no way finished. Skyla
seems to be in her element.

Another five more minutes and she jerks me off. When
Skyla does this, my arousal intensifies, and I can feel myself
ready to reach a climax. I widen my legs to allow her more
access to my phallus. Skyla smiles, as she can feel me going to
explode.The way she builds up her stroke and grips me tighter
is driving me crazy. Skyla knows it will not be long, and she
pulls her bikini top off, exposing her breasts.I rest my hands
on her shoulders as she rests my member on her breasts as her
hand becomes a blur.

Suddenly, Skyla releases me and I cannot stop myself from
unloading all over breasts. Skyla laughs at how much has
poured over her memory glands. She continues squeezing
my shaft to make sure no more can come out. There is a
little dribble and licks my phallus clean.Once she has finished,
she stands up and puts her arms around me, and we kiss
passionately.Before we go to the market, I help Skyla clean
herself in the shower and vice versa.

The market sells trinkets, clothes, souvenirs, beach clothes
and accessories, toys for the beach and fruit stalls. Skyla wants
to buy something to remember her from this place. She also
wants to buy me a gift to say thankyou for taking her to 'Riviera
Maya' and for last night. Not the latte, which was the hardest
job.

Skyla buys a plate with a three-dimensional landscape im-
age of the area. She buys me a wrist band made from rope to
remind me of we had in Mexico.

As it goes dusk, we go to an eatery and have an early dinner
outside in the warm air while witnessing the sun going down.

This is more civilized than last night. No interruptions from the locals and staying sober. We share a bottle of cold crisp Rose with our meal. She had fish with salad and, being a man, steak with boiled, skinned potato and a little salad.

We head back to the villa a little after ten o'clock from the restaurant and choose to walk back and enjoy the long stroll. We joke about our time together over the past three weeks and laugh about how we first met. She thought I was pompous, and I thought she was a entitled.

Skyla still cannot believe I am a millionaire by the way I behave and do not wear an expensive watch or luxury shoes. She thinks my suits are what lawyers or bankers would wear and not a rich man.

When we eventually get back, I go into the kitchen to find more alcohol to drink as a nightcap before going to bed. We both collapse on the sofa and continue menial conversation.

There is no expectation of what tonight will lead to.

I wonder what our lives will be like after we part in our separate ways. 'Will end you up buying your own place, eventually. Regardless if you meet someone or not?'

Skyla has thought little about the future. 'I think I will. I mean, I want to. But, the thought of owning a property and feeling trapped.'

I laugh at her comment. 'But you want to get married and assume you want kids. How trapped can you be?'

Skyla does not see it like that. 'Being married with kids does not trap you. You can be anywhere with your family. When I was with Brad, I pictured myself living here. Now, I am single, I wonder if my future husband is in LA. If I meet a man and he is from another city, I would prepare me to move. Apart from family, there is nothing holding me there. Besides, you met my family. They are all settled down and have their own lives.'

I see where she is coming from, 'Hypothetically speaking. What if I was someone else, and you had no emotional hangups? Would you be willing to move to New York for me?'

Skyla nods her head. 'Yes, I think I would. But they would have to be really special.'

I question what she means. 'How special?'

Skyla thinks hard. 'They would have to make me laugh.'

We continue drinking until the early hours of the morning. This is the most we have been relaxed, which must be since we became a sexual partner. Nothing happens tonight as we are both drunk and we do not feel pressured to finish where we left off.

We fly back Sunday at midday to get back around six o'clock and plan to have an early night. During the flight, we sit in comfortable silence and in our own bubble reminiscence about our stay in 'Riviera Maya'. Skyla tells me it was the best birthday and weekend she has ever had. She also completely forgot to dwell on Brad.We catch each other staring at the other. We smile to ourselves each time the other person realizes.

All I can think about is what we did together. I never thought Skyla was so sexual as a cute girl. Brad was a fool to end it with her. I would not be embarrassed to introduce her to my parents.

When we get back to the villa, we are too tired to think about cooking, so we order a pizza. We have juice with our peperoni pizza as we have had too much alcohol. We are in bed by nine o'clock for another long week.

Company Retreat

♥

Week 4

Since coming back to the villa, there has been no awkwardness and due to work, neither of us has showed intimacy. Mexico has not come up in conversation and feels like a week ago.We are still cooking for each other and making time for conversation. Since we first had our encounter, Skyla has not mentioned Brad and has not wanted to talk about her feelings. I wonder if she has unloaded everything and has no more to say about her relationship ending. Which makes me think she was ready to have a "no strings attach affair". She made it clear she was not ready for another relationship. Considering we are neither each other's type, Skyla probably finds it easier to have a fling with me. Knowing I will not ask to have a relationship with her and she will not fall in love with me.Skyla is sitting at her desk, twiddling with a pencil in between her fingers and staring into space. Skyla cannot take her mind off Richard and how fun she had with him in Mexico. She enjoyed pleasuring him and could not believe how big his phallus was. It turned her on, watching him enjoy being satisfied and hearing him silently moan.

Her mind turns to her company retreat and wonders if they end up sleeping together. She imagines what he could be like in bed and if he can satisfy her as much as he did with his mouth. She thinks about what happened, the more she feels herself being aroused.She wonders how a man who has never been with a woman could be so good at turning her on. Her thoughts make her want him again.Skyla is struggling to focus on work and instead would rather be with Richard and go for a meal or drinks. She is glad they have an additional two weeks together. She has enjoyed his company with Richard. One thing she did not think she would do was form feelings for him. Her heart is still with Brad and so Skyla can not understand why she has a thing for Richard. He is not her type, as she wants a man who has similar likes and interests living in LA.

Eventually, she snaps out of her conundrum and gets her mind to her work.

My team is busy preparing evidence of the employee who stole hundreds of thousand of dollars from the company, for the police. I have no reason to be here apart from showing my presence to represent the firm.While my staff are in one office, I use another office for myself to read through current work completed by my staff. I am finding it hard to focus on the words on the page. They seem to blur into one, and I blame it on Skyla. I can not get her out of my head.Ever since we had our moment, I cannot stop thinking about Skyla and how much I enjoyed being with her. I think she is dazzling, with a great sense of humor. Yes, she is cute and attractive, but I go for brains, core value and common sense. Skyla has those things which I want in a black woman. It so happens she has those qualities, but she is white and lives in LA. If only Skyla could have a twin version of herself in black.

I cannot stop thinking about how much I enjoyed her pleasuring me and the feeling of her breath and tongue on my phallus. The way she enjoyed stimulating me and having the patience to wait half an hour for me to relieve myself. Skyla shocked me when she wanted me to go over her breasts. I was not expecting to take her bikini top off. And when she made sure I had no more to give.Thinking about it is making me solid and now I cannot stand until I can make my member calm down.We are going to her company retreat as her fake husband and wonder if she would want to repeat Mexico. I think about whether she would want to sleep with me and what she would be like in bed. I wonder how it would feel to be inside her and how much of a stamina she would have waiting for me.I realize how long I have been staring into space and force myself to snap out of thinking about Skyla .The dullness in the pit of my stomach is making me realize I must be forming feelings for her. All I can think about is counting the hours until I see her at the villa. The thought of kissing her and the feel of her tongue in my mouth. The feel of touch and the smell of her hair. I wish she were black.

It will be different saying goodbye to her in three weeks' time. We have crossed the friendship line. I am glad they delayed her apartment move in date for a further two weeks.I do not know what the feelings mean, but all I know is I want to keep spending time with Skyla.

Later on in the afternoon, Skyla texts me to say she will come home late tonight. Before I finish reading her message, I assume she wants to avoid me. But, I see a few emojis of sad faces. My heart sank at first and then lit up when realizing she would rather be with me at home.

Skyla's manager has dumped unexpected work, and she wants to make sure she clears her desk before the weekend. She is sad she will not be seeing much of Richard during the week. She added emojis so Richard would not think she was making an excuse to avoid him.

When Friday comes, Skyla wants to brief me on what is going to happen tomorrow at her company retreat. During dinner, Skyla brings up the conversation about tomorrow.

Skyla first apologizes for her absence. 'I would like to say sorry for not being around all this week. A last minute new investment came in and my boss wanted to rush an analysis on it. A new investor came on to our portfolio. I didn't want it looming over my head during our weekend.'I make it clear I was fine, 'It gave me time to hangout with my staff. I treated them to a meal to show my appreciation. All expenses paid for. So, it worked out for both of us.'

Skyla talks about this weekend. 'As I mentioned before, my boss assumed I was married and asked for my husband to come with me. So, I got carried away and said yes without thinking about it. I have said nothing about you, so you can say anything you want. Be yourself and tell him the truth. If he asks how we met, we use the same story as we did when we went out for dinner with your investors. Sound good?'

I am fine with that. 'Yep. No problem.'

Skyla remembers one more thing. 'I did actually tell someone about you. They know the actual truth. Her name is Carla, and she is the one who I got to act as a reference. You remember that?'

I remember, 'Yes. It was the same time you received a text from mum about that family get together we went to. It will be nice to put a face to the name.'

Skyla mentions another thing. 'I said to Carla, if I do not get a proper chance to introduce you to her, she is fine with that. It will be a busy day. But I will point you to her.'

The weekend has come now for the Skyla company retreat. I cannot believe a month has gone by so quickly. This would have been our last week if it was not for work and her delay moving into her apartment.

We have both packed a separate suitcase with evening wear and social clothes for the daytime. She is nervous because she is going to find out if she gets the promotion after this weekend. We have discussed how much she really wants to have the management position. I have asked her to consider the thinking of the future if they do not give her the position. Consider moving to another company for the role.

Skyla is nervous. 'Remember, we are married. We are married. Tell the same story as how we met. Be yourself. The people I work with are cool. You will like them. You will meet my closest friend, Carla. She knows everything and is aware of my lie. Our lie. This means so much to me.'

I reassure her, 'It will be fine. I know how much you want this weekend to go. How do we get there? Limousine, taxi or hire a car.'

Skyla does not want to take the limousine. 'We will get a hire car. My boss does not know you are a millionaire. And he will think I do not need the promotion.'

I think it will be fine, 'We sit with people in admin. I am going to take a less than expensive suit. I'm not taking a tie. They won't notice my wealth.'

Skyla shocks me. 'That is what I love... I mean, like about you. You can blend with anyone. Sometimes it makes me jealous.'

I do not know how to react. 'That is the best compliment I have ever heard. And believe me, I have heard a lot of compliments about from friends.'

Once we are ready to go, we take the limousine to get a ride to a hire company. I think it will be a great idea to hire a luxury car for the weekend as a something fun to do.

We go to Rex Luxury Car Rental at 5250 W Century Boulevard Suite 102.

When we get there, we see a range of cars to choose from between two seaters and four seaters. I want her to decide on a car as it is her weekend.

I quite like the idea of hiring a Ferrari, 'Pick one.'

It fascinated Skyla with the choice of cars. 'I think you should decide.'

I want to go in the car which she would be more excited about. 'You choose one and I'll pay for it.'

Skyla reluctantly walks around, deciding between two cars, 'I think the Maserati.'

I think it is a good option, 'Perfect. I will sort out the paperwork.'

The venue is at the Getty Villa, in Pacific Palisades which is hired out to the company. I let Skyla drive, and she does not need suggesting twice..

When we reach Pacific Coast Highway, Skyla puts her foot down and reaches a hundred miles an hour. I cling on to the door handle as I wonder if I made the right choice.

The wind is loud, and the engine sounds like it is trying to rip through the hood. I can see us taking off from the ground. We weave in between traffic, and Skyla is enjoying the speed and trying to impress me with her driving.

We arrive at the villa around eleven o'clock in the morning and we are one of the first few people here. The noise of the car attracts small attention, but not too much.

We park up and get out our luggage from the trunk and walk along the gravel to the villa.

Skyla wonders how I found her driving. 'You weren't too nervous, were you?'

I smile at her. 'I thought at one time would not slow down when approaching that bus.'

When we get inside, a co-ordinator instructs us to look at room allocation on a floor plan of the villa. We are told to drop our belongings off now and then regroup at the same spot.

Our room is a nice size, but there is a problem which Skyla did not think through with her plan. There is only one bed, a king-size fourposter bed. But, there is a sofa in our room and assume that will be my sleep. Just glad we are only staying one night.

I joke with her, 'So, the sofa is your bed.'

Skyla fakes a laugh. 'Hilarious. We can share a bed. It is wide enough.'

I guess we could. 'I likc to sleep on the right side of the bed.'

Skyla has a surprise face. 'So do I.'

I will not budge. 'I prefer the right side. So you can sleep on the eft side.'

Skyla wants that side. 'Be a gentleman and let me sleep on the right side.'

I still want my side. 'I got us here. So, as a thank you, I am going to sleep on this side.'

Skyla will not budge. 'We will flip for it. Heads, it is you and tails, it's me.'

I do not carry any money, 'I Don't keep cash on me.'

Skyla wonders why that does not surprise her. 'Why doesn't that shock me? How about a credit card?'

I take mine out of my trousers. 'Number side mine, signature side yours.'

I flip the card with my thumb and allow it to fall on the floor. 'Ah. I sleep on the right side.'

Skyla pretends not to care. 'Whatever. I must warn you, I kick my legs out and so if I hit you, I apologize in advance.'

I laugh at her. 'I will put pillows along the middle.'

Skyla is lost for words and unpacks her clothes in the draws and wardrobes in the room. I copy her and do the same.

It is close to lunchtime and the co-ordinator tells us about a seating plan. So, we do not get to sit with admin. I wonder if we will be stuck with her boss, but I think unlikely.

Skyla wonders over to the board to see where we our seat is. When she comes back, she has a scarce expression. I wonder how bad it is.

I guess what the problem is, 'We are not sitting with admin. From the expression of your face, we are on the boss's table.'

Skyla bows her head. 'I am freaking out. He is very good at sus sing out a fake. I am actually shaking.'

I think this will be a significant challenge. 'We fooled your family, right? We can fool anyone. Questions about me, I will answer them.'

Skyla is relying on me for assurance. 'Okay. I will go along with you. I won't talk about us. Wait for them to ask.'

We have a plan and walk to our table. They provide lunch outside in the garden. There are hired waiters providing champagne for reception and I grab two of them for us.

On our table are the more senior employee of the company. There are eight of us at the table, including wives and partners. We keep to ourselves so not to attract attention. The other woman who is fighting for the same promotion is also at our table, and Skyla discreetly points her out to me.

All her colleagues are here now and the garden seems flooded with everyone here. There is laughter and indistinct chatter around us and a pleasant buzz. There is white and red wine on each table with a bottle of water. It is like a wedding reception. I pour out a glass of white for the both of us.

Skyla's worries about being asked questions about her relationship with me, melts away. The conversation on our table turns to enjoying the weekend ahead and laughing about funny moments in their personal life. As I get to know their names and briefly say we are together, our table is relaxing.

Skyla's boss has not come to our table yet and our meals have not arrived yet.

The co-ordinator abruptly sounds her voice on a microphone and asks us to be quiet before the senior manager makes a speech. Everyone stops what they were talking about and turn round to face the front.

Her boss speaks next, 'Hi. My name is Owen. Thank you for all your hard work this year. We have had a bumper year. Now, this weekend is not about discussing work. It is about getting to know you're co-workers and making recent employees feel a part of the team. Also, to allow your husbands, wives and partners what you actually do for work.'

There is quiet laughter from all the tables, including ours.

Owen continues, 'Over the weekend we will have team building games, evening dinner and a prize for the best team player. Now, it is time to serve up lunch. Thank you for your time and enjoy the weekend.'

All of us clap after he finishes his speech. Then walks over to our table.

Owen is Caucasian and in his fifties, with a full head of gray hair. He is six feet tall with a solid frame and olive skin. He is clean shaven with an oblong face.

He is wearing a pair of trousers, shirt and blazer with a hanker chief inside the pocket and no tie.

His personality is bubbly and likes to make people laugh to make them feel at ease. He likes to know about his employees' personal life and their interests. To make them feel a part of the company and important.

He is one of the board members and manages the traders and investment analyst.

After Owen takes a seat next to his wife, he asks everyone is okay with drinks while we wait for the food to come out. He notices Skyla and her competing colleague.

The woman is similar age to Skyla, with brunette hair and similar build. Her name is Kimberley and is keen to make herself noticeable.

Kimberley compliments him on his clothes. 'I like the way you and your wife are color coded. It looks cute.'

Owen is baffled by her comment. 'Skyla, are you going to introduce us to your husband?'

Skyla clears her throat. 'Yes. This is Richard Lewis.'

Owen is confused. 'But your surname is Parker.'

Skyla thinks on her feet, 'I didn't want to lose my family surname. So, I kept mine.'

Owen is old-fashioned, 'I don't get the kids of today. When you got married in my day, you just took your husband's name, regardless.'

Skyla shrugs off his opinion. 'How long have you been married?'

Owen chuckles to himself, 'Long enough. Fifty years. Do you think you last that long? With the youth of today. Easy come easy go.'

Skyla wants to prove they will last the distance. 'We have a lot in common and we are a solid couple.'

Owen wants to challenge her. 'What do you have in common?'

Skyla becomes unstuck, 'Huh. We like the same things.'

Owen backs her into a corner. 'Name me one.'

Skyla tries to think quickly of something realistic. 'We both like hip hop.'

Owen stares at me and then Skyla. 'Richard looks more like a classical guy. He is not exactly dressed like how a hip hop fan would. You guys are in your thirties.'

I give her moral support, 'Eighties hip hop. We don't listen to it anymore. But, it shows we are on the same page. Both of us like to cook for each other. We like fast cars. We even hired a Maserati to get here. And we are both close to our families.'

Owen sees another side to her. 'You like fast cars. You never told me you are into cars.'

Kimberley tries to be more interesting. 'We love doing Origami.'

Owen turns to her with another baffled expression. 'Richard, how did you persuade Skyla to marry you? She is fiercely independent and self sufficient.'

I stare at Skyla and thought of something believable. 'It was easy. We fell in love and she realized she was a better person with me than without me. Which is why you considered her for a promotion.'

Owen and the rest of the guest on the table, except for Kimberley, coo over us. Kimberley hits her husband under the table and we hear the smack. Skyla touches my leg and gives me a quick squeeze and mouths to me, 'thank you'.

Owen puts the same question to Kimberley's partner. 'Seth, how did you persuade Kimberley to marry you? She is fiercely independent and self sufficient.'

Seth struggles to come up with a reason. 'Um. We are better together than alone.'

Owen has a blank expression, wondering what kind of answer was that, 'Okay. Richard, what do you do for work?'

I give the same answer as before: 'I count money all day.'

Owen is the first person to guess right. 'An accountant. Do you work for one of the top three firms?'

I take a sip of wine before answering, 'I actually own my firm.'

Owen's face lights up. 'How many clients do you have?'

I make a hazard guess, 'About five hundred clients. Ranging from as little as twenty thousand dollar turn over to a million.'

Owen is appears impressed, 'You must have some people working for you.'

I play down my business so not to ruin Skyla's chance of promotion, 'Only a hundred employees.'

Owen stares at Skyla. 'You have a catch. I wonder why you are working to get a promotion. Kimberley's husband is an admin worker. I can see why she wants the promotion.'

Kimberley gloats at Skyla and relishes Owen, favoring her for the role.

I feel bad being honest, making her look like she does not need the offer of more money.

Skyla fights why she deserves to the position. 'Yes, my husband has done well for himself. But I am not relying on him to subsidize me. I am too independent to give up my career to be a housewife.'

Owen likes her answer. 'I see why I suggested you could be right for the job.'

On that note, the table briefly goes quiet, and the waiter changes the mood when he gives us our starter.

Decision

♥

After lunch, it is fun and games with three-legged race, egg and spoon race and bicycle polo. Each person has to pair up and stay together for the games. Some couples choose to their co-worker to compete with, but Skyla and I choose to work together.

During the games, we are too competitive, and if we lose; we take it extremely badly. Here, we lose at everything and I think it is to do with focusing on one another. Since the weekend away for her birthday, I feel we are more than a convenience. I think my feelings are growing even though I do not want to take our current closer as we make more eye contact and a few times and feel there is being a connection.

Skyla constantly has a smile on her face, and we never leave our sides.

Come six o'clock, the co-ordinator asks us to get ready for tonight's evening dinner and to wear smart evening wear. Everyone is tired of being out in the sun and playing silly sports all day. I have really had fun today and I hope she has forgotten about the pretense of being a married couple.

I have made a few friends during the afternoon.

We get to our room and I suggest chilling out and having water and coffee before going back for the evening. We have two hours to kill, and it will only take twenty minutes to get ready. So, it leaves us an hour to relax.

I have my back to her as I try to see where the kettle is. 'I'll make us some coffee. Have a glass of water. I feel tipsy and we have the evening to go.'

Skyla does not respond, and I turn round to see if she is okay.

I see she is a bit withdrawn and wonder if the sun and the drinks have got to her. 'You okay? Want to lie down? Get you some water? Is there something on my face?'

Skyla does not respond, but she walks over to me slowly, and I can see her collapsing in my arms from the sun and alcohol. I smile at how cute she looks drunk. I wait for her to reach me so I can help her to the bed to lie down. As I continue smiling and almost laughing at her, she puts her finger on my mouth to stop me and then we have eye contact once again. But this time she plants her lips on mine and it surprises me. I never saw her anymore than a friend. Yes, she is very attractive, and she smells really nice tonight and she tastes of champagne.

Skyla knows she will probably regret doing this, but her feelings have changed for Richard. Yes, she is still getting over Brian and she still loves him, but she has an urge to make a play for Richard.

She closes her eyes as she places her mouth on his and can feel how full his lips are and how soft they are. Skyla can taste his breath, and it is how she imagined it to be. She really wanted to make love to him in Mexico, but did not have the nerve to. But now she does not want to make that mistake a second time. She made sure she drank enough dutch courage to go ahead with making a pass at him. If he rejected her, she can pretend to have no memory of being declined.

However, she finds him reciprocating as she feels him hold her close to his chest and push his gorgeous lips to hers. She recounts the times she caught him in his underwear or in the shower with him noticing and seeing his gorgeous body in the flesh. She found her heart skip a beat when he came out of the pool and seeing the water cascade down his body as he came out of the water.

It has been months since she slept with a man and years since she slept with a genuine gentleman who never once made a pass at her and respected her space. He really listened to her when she wanted a companion. Now, she is curious about what it is like to sleep with a black man and a millionaire with expensive aftershave.

They have been kissing for what seems like ten minutes, but is only a couple of minutes. Already she can feel how stiff my phallus is as her leg presses up against it. She really wants to pull it out as I feel her hands rub the length of me before trying to undo my button to my trousers.

When Skyla reaches down inside Richard's underwear to feel it against her palm and fingers, it feels like the size of a torch. It reminded her of Mexico when feels how rock hard he is. It turns her on, and she feels herself becoming aroused between her legs.

We scuffle and fall on the bed with me on top and I apologize as well as asking if I have hurt her. She ignores me and continues kissing me, occasionally slipping her tongue inside my mouth.

Our passion for one another leaves our emotions running high. We frantically fight to take the other's clothes off to feel closer together.

Skyla catches her breath each time she exhales through her nasal passage and whispers, 'I want you inside me.'

I pause and take a long stare into her eyes. 'Are you sure? You are still getting over Brad.'

Skyla gently signals permission. 'I want you inside me.'

She is gorgeous right now. 'I hadn't realized how dark your eyes are. I could drown in them and I am an excellent swimmer. You have such a cute nose. And your smile is to die for.'

Skyla smiles at me and exhales as I enter inside her. 'Aww. You could have warned me.'

We both laugh as we slowly make love together. I ask her if she is okay as I gently give a rocking motion. After only a couple of minutes, I release myself inside her.

Skyla assumes it is over. 'That's a shame. I thought you would be a gentleman and let me orgasm first.'

Our bodies shudder as we both laugh, and my sensitive member is uncomfortable.

I have not finished though, 'Who says you cannot have your climax?'

Skyla has a quizzical facial expression until I motion my hips. She gasps without warning as I enter inside her. My phallus goes hard again as I feel myself slide into her warm vulva. Skyla asks me to go harder and deeper inside her.

Skyla is still nowhere to reaching her ecstasy and Richard suggests turning her over and lie along her back. Skyla is shocked how stimulated her G spot is and it is the first time she has done this position. She wants him to go faster and harder to agitate her G spot and reach climax sooner.

I follow Skyla's lead and build up a fast rhythm while I hear her breathing grow deeper. I reach underneath her and grab her breasts. Her solid nipples are between my fingers and stimulate them to turn her on more.I raise my chest slightly away from her back to change the angle of my penetration. Eventually, I can feel Skyla's body stiffen and her back arch as she finally reaches nirvana. I hear her moan in relief and continue to slide myself into her as she has multiple orgasm. When she has overcome her orgasm, I hear her burst into laughter, as she cannot believe it worked.I sit up and slowly pull out of her as I watch her twitch and tremor. I admire her bum and savor her musk aroma flow through my nostrils. The scent of her vulva is so welcoming. I lie next to her and rub her back for comfort.

Skyla turns to face me. 'I wanted to do that when we were in Mexico. But I didn't want to force it.'

I confess to her as well, 'I wanted to sleep with you too. But, didn't know if you would be okay with it.'

Skyla puts her arm around my waist. 'This puts a new meaning to pretending to be married.'

Skyla turns on her side and rests her head in her hand.I cannot help fondle her nipple. 'At least we don't have to pretend anymore.'

Skyla has no regrets. 'I am glad I did this. I never thought we would end up like this.'

I am honest with her, 'I never thought for one minute something would happen between us. I thought Mexico would be a one off. '

Skyla uses her fingers to fondle my phallus. 'Does this mean we just have sex until you move into your apartment and I head back to New York?'

Skyla has not thought that far ahead. 'I think so. All week I never thought of Brad once. All I could think of was you and what you would be like in bed. '

I cannot believe she told me that, 'You are so beautiful. I cannot get enough of you.'

Skyla struggles to accept my words. 'You're only saying that now we have slept together.'

I lean forward and kiss her tenderly on her lips. 'I would never have slept with you if I thought otherwise. I really want to stay here rather than go to the evening party.'

Skyla smiles, 'So do I. But I need to make an impression on my boss to get that promotion.'

I agree with her. 'Let's get in the shower and change for tonight.'

We both get in the shower together and wash each other under the waterfall. We cannot keep our hands off each other continue to kiss. It still feels weird that one minute we were good friends, the next minute we are friends with intimacy.

After we finish showering, we change into the bedroom and watch each other change into our evening wear. I watch her put on a pair of black lace thongs and she bends over to pick up her bra and gives me a full view of her behind.

Skyla puts on her bra facing me and watches me put on my underwear, and she is fixated by my manhood as I flip it inside my black briefs. I have a semi hard on watching her change, which she enjoys watching inside my underwear.

Skyla asks me to zip the back of her black dress and pushes her bum against my groin on purpose. I get instantly aroused and feel myself nudge between the crack of her bum through her dress.

Once we are both ready, let her walk out first and walk behind her.

Dinner was nice, and we continued to have banter at the table with the same guests. We feel like we are the center of attention and I kept the humor going.

Kimberley and her husband felt like they were struggling to show their warm side.

After dinner finishes, Skyla and I decide to get stronger drinks at the bar. We excuse ourselves and tell them we will meet them during the award ceremony.

While we wait at the bar to be served, her boss, Owen, walks up behind us and acknowledges himself. We both turn round to make conversation.

Owen sees something different to us. 'You two seem reju-venated. The hot shower here can do that.'

Skyla laughs. 'Having a lie down and a shower has helped.'

Owen can see that, 'Maybe my wife and I should have had that lie down as well.'

I burst into laughter. 'Sorry. It is something that I remember from this afternoon.'

Owen reminds us of our performance, 'Even though you lost every game, you seemed happy just to be a team together. You two never stopped laughing and smiling. I think you two were somewhere else.'

Skyla blushes. 'We were enjoying taking part rather than trying to win.'

Owen puts his hand over my shoulders. 'Where have you been hiding him? If I had known you were this fun outside of work, I would have promoted you a long time ago. Maybe he should come and work for me, to make your personality shine in the office.'

Skyla is open-mouthed, 'If I had known that, I would have introduced you to him weeks ago.'

Owen is confused. 'Weeks ago? I am talking years ago.'

Skyla realizes what she has said. 'I mean, I would not have waited until today to introduce you to him.'

Owen shrugs his shoulders. 'See you on the dance floor.'

Skyla cannot believe what Owen said, and we celebrate by downing a couple of shots of 'Snake Bites'. Then wait for the award to be announced.

We hear someone come on the mike on stage and assume it is time to find out who wins tonight. I assume it will be someone who won this afternoon. The couple that won with the highest points were a young couple who were probably graduates in their first year of work. They were very compet-itive. I felt they needed to take a chill pill.

During the long speech talking about how the couple, despite losing, never stopped their outlook on life; I suggest to Skyla we should go for a walk or go back to the room. Skyla smiles and playfully hits me, thinking it is a code for more sex. She pulls my arm around her waist and enjoys my warm company.

Owen now comes up on stage and Skyla shh's me. 'I hope you guys and girls have had a great day.'

Everyone cheers and claps to acknowledge they had fun.

Owen continues, 'This award goes to a couple that I had the privilege of getting to know. Despite there not being enough wine on the table and being the butt of all jokes, they never let it get them down. They made everyone laugh and feel be part of the conversation. Out of all the couples here, including my wife and I, they were unmistakably clear that they were the happiest couple here today. You would think they were newlyweds, the way they behaved today. You two put the rest of us to shame and after tonight, I will get advice from you on how to make my wife happy.'

There is further laughter and jeering before allowing him to finish his speech.

Owen goes to raise his glass, 'Without further a do, I would like to announce the winner of this year's retreat.'

Skyla is leaning towards my idea of finding somewhere private to be intimate. She suggests going for a walk in the garden. As we go to leave, Owen goes to announce the lucky couple.

Owen peers into the crowd to see where the couple is. 'Please, can you put your hands together for Mr. and Mrs. Lewis and Parker?'

We stop in our tracks and wonder if we heard correctly as we did not win a thing at games today, and we were just being ourselves.

Her colleagues chant our names and we awkwardly walk over to the stage to collect the award from Owen.

Both of us are speechless and question him if they got the right couple. Owen laughs, thinking we were being modest and polite. We genuinely think they made a mistake. Owen expects us to make a brief speech.

Skyla and I glance at each other, wondering who is going to say something.

Owen makes that choice, 'Mr. Lewis is going to make a speech. Come on here.'

I turn to Skyla, embarrassed, and she gives me encouragement to go up to the mike and make a speech.

I feel like someone have thrusted me into the limelight, 'Not sure if anyone can hear me. I am normally quiet.'

The audience laugh thinking I was trying to be funny.

I smile while they laugh. 'Wow. I don't think we deserve this. The couple with the highest score should be here. But I don't think you would allow that.'

There is more laughter when I was not trying.

I take my time thinking of a speech befitting for this award. 'I would like to thank Owen for the compliment of giving the perception of living like it is our first year of marriage. Trust me, we work hard at it every day. It does not come easy to us but one thing we swear by. Make each day count as if it is your last. Don't take each other for granted and life is too short to wallow in sadness. It is true, we behave like we only met four weeks ago. But it really feels that way. When I met Skyla, she was in a bad way. I mean, she was miserable. Her previous boyfriend let her go. Can you believe that? Just look at her.'

Everyone claps again and goes 'awww' in unison.

I turn to Skyla. 'How can you turn away a face like that? She even looks cute when she blushes, like she is doing right now. Did Skyla ever tell you how we met?'

The crowd all say no.

I tell them a half truth, 'For those who don't know, I came into town only for a business trip. I hired a villa because that's what I do when I see clients outside of New York. Well, I booked this villa, and it was double booked by mistake. We both got a shock when I came out to the swimming pool outside and she was in a very nice swim suit and just happened to be topless.'The audience cheers.I continue the story. 'We both scared each other.'

Everyone laughs and I wait for them to go quiet again.

I think about the time when we got to know each other. 'She put on a cold front with an attitude. She was adamant that she had rights to the villa. We locked horns, and she embarrassingly realized I was right. She got flustered and embarrassed.'I pause for a second and admire her standing next to me.I realize what she does when she is nervous 'Have you ever noticed she scratches her neck when she is nervous? Well, that is how we met. I allowed her to stay. After a month of annoying each other and her getting over her ex-boyfriend. Something happened. I'm not sure if I believe in fate or god was looking out for us, but we suddenly realized we liked each other. I won't go into detail about what happened after that.'

The crowd laugh again after realizing what I mean. Skyla goes bright red, which makes them laugh even more.

I finish the speech. 'It was not then when I realized I loved her. It was that. Right there. Her smile. I made a bet with myself. If I could make her smile through all the hurt and pain she was going through, I would have her. And that is what happened. When we got married, we couldn't wait. We did not have our parents there. We didn't even have our friends. It is the only thing we regret. We eloped because we could not wait a week, a month, a year to get married. The other regret is that we didn't have a first dance.'

Again the crowd goes 'awww'.

A man on a piano unexpectantly reacts, 'I would like to announce Mr. and Mrs. Lewis and Parker first dance.'

I do not know what I was saying and kept ongoing until I could reach a closure. Skyla found me amusing and now we have to dance for our wedding that never took place.

I help her from the stage on to the dance floor. They made room for us and the pianist makes up a tune to suit the mood. As we have our first slow dance together, the crowd slowly chants quietly for us to kiss.

Skyla and I stare at each other, wondering whether to bow to their request. Skyla and I awkwardly wonder whether to go for a kiss. Making love was spontaneous, and it was natural. Now, feel forced.

I awkwardly move my mouth to hers and wait for her reaction. She does not hesitate and we tenderly kiss. The crowd cheer us on as we lose ourselves and make a lingering kiss, forgetting where we are.

Soon after the dance, we feel embarrassed and go outside to deflect the attention.

We go for a stroll in the lovely garden and have a thought-provoking conversation.

I have had a great day, very different from my normal life. 'Thank you for asking me to come. I've had a great time. Your coworkers are great. They have a good heart. I noticed Carla was tearful when she saw us dance.'

Skyla is thrilled and holds my hand. 'I noticed too. She seems to think we are suited. I am glad I you came. My boss hinted to me I will get the promotion. After you went to use the bathroom.'

I am happy for her and see her getting the role. 'You will start a new beginning and find the love of your life.'

Skyla goes quiet. 'Since breaking up with Brad, I have been reflecting on my life. Wondering what it is I want out of life. When I was in school, we did a project about Tahiti. I told myself I would go traveling there when I graduated. But they offered me a job and felt I would not get another opportunity like that.'

We reach a statue and I sit on the edge of the base, which is waist level.

I see she has a dilemma. 'I remember you telling that story.'

Skyla racks her brain. 'Of course. I did. Dah.'

I ask her a question, 'So, what is it you want to do now?'

Skyla is at a loss. 'I don't know. I want the job, but wonder if getting the travel bug out of my system will also help me find myself again. Also, decide what I want to do with the rest of my life.'

I want to know if she has decided, 'Will you go traveling or choose the job?'

Skyla makes a choice. 'If I get the job, and I take it, I will never go traveling. And I will regret it. But, I want to own my house one day. It will set me back if I leave.' I feel for her as I can see her eyes, she is in a conundrum.

It is getting late, and we decide to retire to our room. The remaining evening will be dance and more drinks.

We avoid the dance scene by going into the house through another entrance to get to our bedroom. We can still hear the faint noise of the music and instinct chatter.

I stare at the bed and think about what we did earlier. It feels serial now we are behaving like friends. Assuming Skyla does not want to blur the lines again, I automatically choose the sofa.

Skyla watches me preparing for sleep and going to the sofa. 'I thought we were going to share the bed. You won the flick of a card and you get the right side.'

I still think she wants no more headache in her life. 'I was just sitting here before heading to bed.'

Skyla changes into her sleep wear, which tells me she does not want a repeat performance.

Lying next to her under the bedsheets reminds me too much of what we did and want to have some more. I feel myself getting anxious and effecting my sleep.

Skyla is trying to sleep, but she cannot stop thinking about how much Richard made her feel. Her urge for sexual attention grows. She wants to do it again, but does not know how to broach the subject. Her thoughts about how nice he smelled and how defined his body is, aroused her. The way he reads her body signal. And being able to continue after already having an orgasm.

I cannot stop thinking about how nice it was to make love to her and reenact in my head what happened. The feeling of being inside and inside her felt great.

I cannot contain my urge, 'Skyla?'

Skyla keeps her back to me. 'Yes?'

I hesitate at first, 'I really want to be inside you.'

Skyla reaches behind her and finds my member. 'You're right. It wants to go inside me.'

I quietly laugh, 'You can see, or shall I say feel, how much I want you.'

Skyla frantically pulls her pajama bottom down with her underwear and allows me to enter inside her.

She is so tight; it stimulates me intensely, making me want to cum inside her quickly again.

Skyla cannot believe how she is not getting enough of his manhood. She does not want this moment to end. She motions him to go on top of her while she lies on her front. Also, pulls his hands to grab her breasts and squeeze them. She then raises her bum slightly to allow him to get in deeper.

Skyla wants me to ride her hard on top of her, and I allow her to take the lead. I squeeze her breast, having her nipples between my fingers. I can feel they are solid, like wooden dowels.

Skyla can feel herself reaching orgasm again and thrusts against Richard to heighten the intensity and cums all over his shaft. She feels him building up the pace, pulling almost out and then thrusting inside her with all his might. She tightens her muscles around his shaft as she comes to climax.

As I pump her harder and harder, I feel myself cum, and I cannot delay myself from ejaculating. Just as I cum, I hear Skyla cum at the same time and I keep pounding her to extend her orgasm. Skyla laughs, not quite believing that she came twice in one night. She has never had a man make her cum this frequently.

Skyla cannot think of a time when Brad made her orgasm this much during sex. It was only occasionally through foreplay. Skyla wonders what separates Richard from Brad and her other relationships.

When I feel Skyla cannot go any longer, I roll over to lie next to her. We both snuggle against each other, and I assume this will be the last time we make love.

Skyla pulls my arm across her stomach and places her fingers between mine, and closes them. We both eventually fall asleep.

Family Awkwardness

♥

Week 5

A few days pass and we say nothing about what happened at the weekend. Things resume back to normal, with both of us having busy work commitments.

I feel my work will end as scheduled at the end of next week.

No one who I work with knows about the retreat and what happened as I like my life private. Skyla seems to be the same, even though we have not formally agreed to do so.

While I am in the client's offices overseeing the installation of new software being implemented by my investors, I cannot help gaze into the distance and think about our intimacy.

Skyla is at her desk day dreaming about the weekend. She sees Richard in a different light and cannot stop thinking about the weekend. Her thoughts have moved from Brad to Richard. While she stares past her monitor thinking about him, her boss stands behind her.

Owen has some good news. 'Can you come into my office?'

His presence startled Skyla. 'Oh. I was in deep thought about a company you asked me to look into.'

She follows behind him to his office.

Owen sits behind his desk, motioning Skyla to take a seat herself. 'I saw little you in the evening. Did you have too much to drink?'

Skyla thinks of an excuse. 'I felt tired and had an early night. All that excitement.'

Owen gets down to it. 'I asked you here to say you got the job. Well, what are you going to say?'

Skyla's lost for words. 'Wow, I was not expecting you to come up with a decision before Friday.'

Owen did not take long to come up with a decision. 'After the weekend, I saw something I never saw in you before. A woman who, despite the odd, carried on smiling and enjoying the day.'

Skyla is not sure what he is getting at. 'What are you trying to say?'

Owen wants a cool, level-headed person. 'You didn't lose you cool. You fought as hard as you could, but didn't take it personally. That is what kind of person I am looking for. Can still be bubbly to keep up moral.'

Skyla wonder if that was because of Richard. 'Yes, that's me. I don't know what to say? Have you told Kimberley?'

Owen does not want her to worry about that. 'That is not your concern. You start your new role in a week's time.'

Skyla leaves his office, pleased with the outcome she thought she lose to Kimberley. She thought her boss wanted someone like her who is cold and focused on making money.

Skyla wants to celebrate tonight with Richard and champagne. It is the first person who enters her mind.

As I walk through the front door, Skyla has made dinner already, which I was not expecting. She is in an excellent mood and wonders what happened at work.

Skyla even has champagne glasses on the table and assumes she gets the promotion. I wait for her to tell me what the special cause is for.

I ask, 'What is the special occasion?'

Skyla opens the bottle. 'I was thinking about how much work I have on today. Staring into space. Then, Owen startles me and I think I am in trouble. Then he calls me into his office. I am thinking it is bad news. He never calls me into the office. Then, he tells me I got the job! Would you believe it?'

I am direct, 'Yes. And the long hours, early start and the times you moan about poor efficiency and workflow, it was obvious.'

We clink glasses and drink before having dinner.

When finish eating we go on the sofa and continue drinking the last of the bottle.

I tell her about a phone call I had with my brother about a family get together including a barbeque. She snuggles closer up against me and asks when it is.

I hesitate to say, 'This weekend is coming up.'

Skyla turns her head to glance up at me. 'Whats the problem? You need a fake girlfriend like I did with my family?'

I sarcastically laugh, 'Ha ha ha. No. But they are going to bug me by asking why I have met no one. I am only the sibling who has not married and had kids.'

Skyla can obviously see her situation in mine. 'If you want me to come with you, ask.'

I wonder what she will do while I am away. 'What will you do?'

Skyla shrugs her shoulder. 'Watch TV all day. Drink out your champagnes and wines.'

I feel sorry for her being here alone for the entire weekend. 'If you want to come instead of being here alone in the villa, it is fine.'

Skyla does not want to come by inviting herself. 'I will only come if you want me to come. I don't want to invite myself if you prefer to be alone.'

I have a rethink and actually want her there, 'I would prefer you there. But I don't want you as a girlfriend or a wife. Just act like what we really are. Good friends.'

Skyla can see how her situation is totally different to my, 'Of course. Your family will be nothing like mine. They know you will meet someone.'

I let her know where the family get together is. 'It is in New York.'

Skyla raises herself up and faces me. 'New York. Never been there. Can we go on the Empire State Building? The Statue of Liberty?'

I roll my eyes. 'We won't have time. We fly there on Saturday and back on Sunday.'

Skyla sulks, 'At least get to see the outside of them.'

I smile, 'From the air.'

Come the Saturday we leave LA after ten o'clock in the morning and arrive in New York close to four o'clock at 'New York Private Jet Rentals & Charters' at 118 W 114th St 1W. We take a taxi to 21 West 33rd Street, where my family will be.

When we arrive, it blows Skyla away when we stop outside the 'Empire State Building'.

Skyla wonders why I did not tell her. 'I thought we did not have time to make visits.'

I tell her why we are here, 'I have made a reservation here. We can go to the top after dinner. We are going to STATE Grill and Bar. Happy now?'

Skyla still moans, 'Will never see the "Statue of Liberty".'

You cannot please everyone and we go inside.

The restaurant is empty, and it puzzled Skyla to why it feels so scarce.

I give her an explanation, 'I hired the place out so it is only family.'

Skyla is stunned. 'How did that cost?'

The average income was based on a Saturday. 'I made some negotiation. I asked to look at their book-keeping and took an average of one month on a Saturday. They take home around tcn thousand dollars. I added twenty percent on top.'

Skyla laughs. 'Wow. You are good.'

We walk up to the table where my family was and introduce Skyla to them. I have three brothers and two sisters who are having their own careers and all live in the New Jersey area. When we reach our table, I introduce Skyla to my family and extended family at the end of the table.

I point to each member of the family, 'Noland, Stefon, Lamonte, Jada and Laila. My brother and sisters. And their kids. My mum and dad.'

There is someone who I do not recognize and is not a part of our family.

I walk over to the woman while Skyla stays standing at the top of the table.

She introduces herself. 'My name is Nova. I am a friend of your brother and work at the same place as him.'

I assume she means Lamonte sat next to her. 'I assume you know who I am.'

Nova smiles, 'Yes. Your brother invited me and thought you may need company. But it looks like you already have a plus one.'

I am puzzled at first, then realize she meant Skyla. 'Oh. She is a friend. She had a spare time in her schedule.'

Nova is a black African woman who I find attractive and wonder if she could be interested in someone like me. There is an empty chair next to her. I see a server going pass and ask if he can have an extra chair. There is not a spare seat for Skyla, as I did not mention to my family I was bringing anyone.

During dinner, Skyla makes small talk with my sister Laila, who is eating next to her. I cannot stop staring in her direction as she smiles and jokes with my sibling. All the while having a conversation with Nova learning about what she does for a living at the same place as my brother and where she lives. I half listen and guest the other half she is saying while I am distracted by Skyla enjoying herself without me.

I kind of feel jealous she is not relying on me to make her feel welcome or keep her company. She is completely ignoring my eye glances like she is in a world of her own.

Nova notices and I quickly ask what her family is like and if she has any siblings.

When dinner is finishing, we have arranged music and dancing. Also, the chance to ride up to the top to view the city. Nova stays with me continuing conversation and my sister whisks Skyla away from eye view.

I should be grateful for a black woman showing interest in me. 'Would you like another drink?'

Nova comes with me, 'I notice you looking over at your friend. Is something going on between you two?'

I naturally lie, 'No. She has never met my family. Worried she will be overwhelming.'

Nova is confident she is fine. 'She is okay. Ignore her. You're with me.'

I smile politely but I dislike her tone. 'If she is worried, she will come and find me.'

Skyla is enjoying Laila's company and learning about Ricard, but she has noticed how he has constantly looked over at her. She found him cute for doing that. She did not want to reciprocate as he is with another woman who she believes likes him. Skyla does not want to ruin Richard's chance of happiness being with a black woman.

However, she feels hurt and cannot understand why. She is curious about who Richard is talking to and wishes he was keeping her company. But she has found that his sister has made her feel very welcome.

Skyla sips a glass of wine while standing next to his sister and gazing at Richard and wondering why she fascinates by him speaking to another woman. Her other thought is to have another intimacy moment when they get back or even on the plane. Their time together so far pops into her head and she cannot help smiling to herself. She thinks about his package and how much she enjoyed pleasuring him and vice versa. The thought makes her less envious of his attention taken by someone else. Skyla now feels she has the upper hand and is spiteful for thinking like this. Her having him at the end of the night and not her.

It frightens her as she has never had thoughts like these about a man in her life, not even Brad. But Richard is making her think like this.

Nova is showing her interest in meeting up after tonight. 'I was wondering if you fancy going for a coffee sometime.'

I think of my work schedule: 'I have to fly back to LA tomorrow. I am away for a week. Then I'm finished. I can meet up when I get up. Take you out for dinner or I can cook for you.'

Nova smiles and likes the sound of that. 'I would love that. You cook for me.'

It is now after nine o'clock and Nova has to leave abruptly and we exchange numbers on our cell phones. Nova rings my number to make sure we have not typed them wrong.

After Nova leaves, my brother Lamonte comes over to talk to me. I know he will want to know what I think about Nova.

Lamonte grips my shoulder behind me. 'So, what did you think of Nova?'

I take a think, 'She is nice. She is my kind of person. I find her attractive. She asked me to go for a coffee. I offered her dinner.'

Lamonte goes giddy. 'I thought she would be your type. So, you're going to take her out?'

I tell him about what we agreed, 'She is going to come to my place and I am going to cook for her.'

Lamonte gives me praise. 'Great. You know how to cook, right?'

I shake my head and smile, 'I'm a superb cook.'

Lamonte is happy for me, and we finish talking. I go to find Skyla.

I see Skyla by herself, holding a glass of wine, and she is staring at the floor in a trance. As I go to give her company, my mum comes up to me to talk.

Mum touches my arm to get my attention. 'How have you been? Not seen you in ages.'

I get flustered wanting to go up to Skyla. 'I'm good. Been busy with work. In LA at the moment.'

Mum wants to know who I was talking to. 'Who is the woman you were with?'

I go shy, not wanting to tell her about my personal life. 'She was nice.'

Mum wants to know more, 'What's her name?'

I am abrupt, 'Nova.'

Mum smiles, waiting for more information. 'What does she do for a living? Is she your type?'

I really do not want to say anymore, 'She is a lawyer. And I'm not sure if there will be anymore to it.'

Mum wants to continue asking questions but I politely stop her and promise to find her belief tonight finishes.

Skyla notices me coming over and snaps out of her gaze, and gives me a gentle, warm smile. 'How are you? I noticed you getting friendly with that girl.'

I play it down. 'She had some interesting things to say. She is a lawyer. So, I might ask her to provide her services.'

Skyla sees through me. 'Is that the type of woman you want to marry? She is very attractive. Compared to me.'

I do not compare them, 'She is doable.'

Skyla smiles, 'Doable? As in sex?'

I mean something else, 'She is girlfriend material.'

Skyla appears sad. 'So, one more week and you go back to your life here.'

I never thought about it. 'Yes. That would be right. We should have a farewell party. Just the two of us. Let's go up top and see the city.'

The view of New York City from 'Empire State Building' is magnificent. You never tire of it. Skyla finds it breathe taking, and she behaves like a child again. I focus on watching her reaction prefer her view than the city.

I walk behind her. 'So, are you happy now you have been to the building?'

Skyla gets distracted by the lights. 'This is great. Do you remember "Sleepless In Seattle"?'

I vaguely remember it. 'Is it where they are supposed to meet? They almost miss each other?'

Skyla turns round to face me and takes my hand. 'And I believe they kissed.'

Our eyes lock once again, and Skyla moves backwards against the wall, showing the view. I find myself drawn to her and kiss passionately. She puts her arm around my neck and I grab her from around the waist. I pull away to have a view of her face and body to create lasting memories before sinking my lips into hers again and squeeze her so tight; I do not want to let go.

Something about her makes me want to do things to her. Skyla is not in a hurry to end our encounter and she reaches down to my trousers and fumbles her hand inside my sip and feels for my groin. I feel her perfectly round bum and squeeze.

Skyla pulls away and sees who is around before going down on her knees and pulling it out. I feel the cool air and her warm breath on me and it feels great. I am afraid someone will see us in a particular family. But, the sensation and watching Skyla concentration on her face as she slides her tongue and mouth along my length and then raising it up to reach my balls. She really knows how to turn me on.

I want to satisfy her but I do not have the courage to give her foreplay in public like this.

Eventually, I feel myself reaching a climax and beg her to stop before I make a mess of both of us. There is no way we can try to clean up the mess without being noticed and that it will leave a stain on my trousers.

I warn her of climax, 'You gotta stop. Right now, I will cum. I don't want to leave a mess on your dress or get it in your hair.'

Skyla is not listening to me as she continues to pleasure me. As soon as she takes me in her mouth and watches her gorgeous head bob up and down in a slow, seductive motion, it sends me over the edge. Without warning, I ejaculate and, by surprise, she takes the lot in her mouth and does not allow any of it to go on our clothes or on her face and hair. She continues to suck until my body stops to spasm and stiffen.

Skyla gently pops it back in my trousers and smiles at me. 'I bet Nova couldn't do that with you?'

I am in disbelief and speechless. 'I cannot believe you just done that. And in view of anyone coming round the corner.'

Skyla ignores my concern, and we return to kiss passionately. 'I think we should return to the group. They could wonder where you are.'

I vaguely pay attention to her suggestion and let her take the lead.

Birthday Boy

♥

When we get back to the restaurant, one of my other brothers comes up to me. Skyla goes to get another drink and leaves us to talk. It intrigued Stefon to know who I am with.

Stefon waits for her to be out of earshot. 'What is happening? You're not wearing a tailor suit. There is a silly pattern to the tie you are wearing. You're not uptight and wondering when it is time to go.'

I laugh off his observation. 'It is a social event.'

Stefon wants to know how I know her. 'How did you two meet? She is not exactly the type you would normally go for. Not that you have ever invited someone to a family to do.'

I laugh nervously this time. 'We are just friends. I am renting out a villa while working in LA. There was a mixup with the booking, and she thought it was her accommodation for the month. Out of pity, allowed her to stay. She had nothing to do, so I invited her here. No big deal.'

Stefon jokes, 'Not being funny, but if I was not married with kids, I would work on that. Even though she is not black.'

I cringe at the thought. 'Well, you are married and she is a person. She is a woman, and in fact, works on the stock exchange. As an analysis.'

Stefon has a different view. 'Well, she is both very attractive, sexy and intelligent. She reminds me of "Cameron Diaz". But, with long hair and a tighter behind. Do have feelings for her?'

I question his interest. 'Why would you want to know if I like her?'

Stefon sees something. 'You look like a pair of couples. I thought she was your girlfriend for a sec. Wondered why you were chatting up the other woman.'

I do not mention our arrangement to meet up. 'She was talking to me. I felt obliged to make conversation with her. She was alright. Did anyone else ask about Skyla?'

Stefon burst out laughing. 'Mum and dad almost fell over when you came in with a woman. They almost got whip lashed taking a double take.'

I sarcastically laugh. 'Hilarious. Seriously. Any negative comments?'

Stefon is serious now. 'No. Everyone thought you finally met someone. Surprised she was white. As it fixated you with being pro black. They are thinking she could be the one you end up marrying.'

I shrug off his comment. 'If I brought a white girl home, the family would get funny.'

Stefon thinks something could be real. 'If that is the girl you end up wanting to be with. All that matters is you are happy. The problem is getting on with her side of the family. Are they like the Kardashian's?'

I roll my eyes. 'What are you talking about?'

Stefon jokes, 'They are into their black men.'

I sigh. 'Her family is normal. They are actually pretty decent. Each of her of siblings married into other cultures. They thought we were boyfriend and girlfriend. They made me feel welcome.'

Stefon quickly reassures me, 'And we do as well. Laila thought that you two were boyfriend and girlfriend. All Skyla said was good things about you. She couldn't stop getting the dirt on you. Previous girlfriends, whether that girl was your type and what you were like before you became a millionaire?'

I am shocked, 'You're kidding me. What did our sister say?'

Stefon remembers snippets, 'She told her the time when you went as a stockbroker to one Halloween party. Including briefcase and braces. And here you are with a stockbroker.'

I correct him, 'An analysis. She does not actually work on the floor in the bull pit. She researches on the next big thing coming on the market.'

Skyla is coming back with both our drinks, and I hush my brother. She thinks we are acting weird and wants in on the joke. I tell her it is a family long running joke.

The evening finishes after nine o'clock in the morning and we stay on until everyone has safely caught a taxi. Then Skyla and I find our taxi to head back to my place.

Skyla is keen to see what my house looks like and forgot we were not going back tonight, as it is a late night.

We arrive at my house around eleven o'clock and she is stunned that I live in a residential area and not some enormous mansion gated with stone walls like my investment in LA.

Once inside the reception area, I ask her what she thinks of the place.

Skyla can only see the living area from the front door, but already has an opinion. 'It feels like a showroom. Everything in its place. No dust or scrunched cushions. Have you ever sat on the furniture?'

I find us some wine to drink and two glasses. 'What do you mean? The creases obviously fell out from not being sat in for weeks.'

Skyla laughs at my reasoning. 'You tell yourself that. Wow! Your back yard looks amazing. Now I know why you chose this place. You have a swimming pool in your back garden with like a roof. Is it heated?'

I pour out two glasses while nodding my head. 'I spent a fortune renovating this place. It cost my about a hundred grand. Now it is worth around a mill. Spent another hundred grand getting just how I wanted it. It was the worst house on the street. The neighbors wanted it ripped down because it was an eye sour. Put up a huge fence during construction. When finished, the neighbors wanted to have the same thing done.'

Skyla finds it shocking to how big the house is. 'I thought it was just the reception and living area. You have a whole another house back here. How big is the garden?'

I have a estimated idea, 'Not totally sure. Probably two acres. Not much really.'

Skyla's blowing her mind. 'I wonder why you do not have a wife. I would snap you up if I came here on a date.'

I stare at her how much she cute complimenting the house. 'Believe it or not. You're the first girl I have brought here. Or shall I say, woman?'

Skyla takes her glass of wine. 'Wow. If it was me, I would have found you a long time ago to bring you here. Don't let any woman take residence here.'

I find her sincere, 'I told myself that the first woman I brought her, I would end up marrying.'

Skyla almost crooks her neck when she turns round. 'I wish I was that woman. This place is gorgeous.'

I appreciate her words, 'Well, if you're ever in town, you are more than welcome to stay here. I even have a wine cellar. But, nothing is expensive. Saves going to the liquor store.'

Skyla jokes about having to share the same bed. 'I don't think your wife would approve of the three of us staying in the same bed.'

I laugh, 'Don't worry. It is a seven-bedroom house. You can have the last bedroom on the other end.'

Skyla pokes her tongue out. 'Is my room already prepared?'

I have to think for a moment, 'All my beds have fresh bedding. You can choose anyone.'

Skyla jokes with him, 'So, I can choose your bed?'

I smile and think to myself, she will be the first woman in my bed, 'I like my bed too much to give it to you.'

Skyla is direct. 'How about I let you sleep in your bed while I sleep in it?'

I obviously want to be with her tonight. 'I sleep on the right side.'

Skyla laughs, remembering her retreat. I put my wine down on the side table and walk over to her and cannot stop myself from holding her face and kiss her. Skyla pulls away and takes a long look at my fae before going in for a kiss.

Skyla does not hold back. 'Take me to bed and lose me in your arms.'

The next day we wake up and have pillow talk about what the last week will be like. She asks me if I think Nova could be the one. I brush it off not understanding. I only met her last night, and we did not fall over each other.

Skyla teases me. 'You are falling for her. What is it? She is gorgeous, black and a lawyer. That is what your sister said.'

I wonder if she has forgotten about Brad. 'And how about you? Anyone you like?'

Skyla appears withdrawn from the question. 'Maybe. There is a guy at work who I might like. He is not as rich as you, but he is a gentleman. He keeps offering to cook for me. Like you, he has listened to my problems and even though I must have sounded like a broken record, he kissed me. Only this week.'

I am stunned and feel a kind of jealous, 'Why didn't you tell me? I would have backed away from you. Give your heart a chance to pursue him.'

Skyla nervously smiles, 'Because we are still here until the end of next week. I want to wait until this has finished.'

Skyla is lying about meeting a new man. The person she is describing is Richard. She realizes she is jealous that he has potentially found his future partner after only one encounter. She thinks they instantly hit it off.

Before we head straight to the airport, I take a detour with the taxi to the 'Statue of Liberty'. I thought I would make it a surprise for Skyla to have her buck list ticked. We go up to the top and see the skyline of the city. We stay for a couple of hours before we head back to Los Angeles.

We arrive back in LA after six o'clock and both of us are exhausted. We do little and decide to order food in rather than try to cook.

A couple of days later, I come back from work and I see flowers on the table in the livingroom and assume it is from the guy Skyla mentioned on Sunday. It jolts my heart, realizing she has met someone else.

Skyla walks in after hearing the door open. 'Your're back. You never told me it was your birthday today. I got back from work and saw them at the front door. I thought you bought them for me. For a moment, I was worried.'

I do not know who it is from. 'I assumed it was from your new admirer. No one knows I am here. And, I do not celebrate my birthday. Did you see who it is from?'

Skyla chose not to check. 'I thought I would wait for you to get home. Aren't you going to check?'

I pull the card from the top centre of the flowers and chuckle to myself, 'You won't believe this. It is from Nova.'

Skyla has a deflated expression, 'How come she found out about your birthday?'

I wonder myself, 'Lamonte must have told her. It was he who invited her to our family get together. He must have given her the idea of how to get my attention.'

Skyla wonders why none of his family told her, 'If I had known, I would have brought you something.'

I feel wanted for the first time in my life. 'It is sweet. But it is not like she bought me an expensive gift. Not that I want someone to spend money on me. If I wanted you to do something for me, I would have told you.'

Skyla is sorry for me. 'You never celebrated your birthday. Why did you make a fuss of mine?'

I knew she liked to be spoiled on her birthday. 'That is what you like, so I gave you what I knew would make you happy. I don't enjoy being fussed over.'

Skyla sends out the feelers. 'If you were married now, what would you want to do on your birthday with your wife? On the assumption she insisted on doing something for you?'

I see what she is doing. 'I would ask what she wanted to do for the day.'

I irritate Skyla about clamming up and she says she has to go out for a while. I know she is going to return the favor and buy me a cake.

A while later, as predicted, she brings back a cake and a couple of packs of candles. I begrudgingly accept and we share a quarter of the cake. It is close to ten o'clock and I am ready for bed. I have an early start and so I want to be alone.

Skyla respects my wishes and goes into her own bedroom.

The next morning, I wake up from the alarm at five o'clock in the morning. I aim to leave by six o'clock to be in the newspaper office to go over a final report on the financial transactions. And check, we have enough evidence to support fraudulent theft from the company to put away one of its employees.

I have my usual toast and coffee, and I am quiet so not to disturb Skyla. I thought she would be up all ready to go to work, but she was still in her bedroom. As I am about to leave for work, Skyla appears from her bedroom in pajamas still.

Skyla does not seem to go to work today. I wonder what she has planned for today and why she never told me. I do not give it a second thought and go to leave. She asks why I am leaving for work, which I find strange.

I turnaround and ask her why, 'What are you doing today?'

Skyla has other ideas. 'I spoke to a Simon, your senior employee? I told him about it being your birthday yesterday and he told me he didn't know. So, I asked if you could have tomorrow off. As a late birthday. Naturally, he said you do not need to be there today.'

I want to read the report before they pass it on to John. 'I need to be in the office. Before they give the document to the client, I have to look over it.'

Skyla shows any interest. 'Well, I told him and he seems to think it is all in hand. So, you're taking the day off and I have plans for you.'

I have wasted time waking up early, 'Well, I own the company. What do you have in mind? Mexico?'

Skyla smiles and giggles. 'Not as extravagant by my salary. But I did some digging myself.'

Once she changes into a black flowing dress, she takes us in the limousine.

Last Night

Skyla keeps her surprise closely guarded in her chest. We hold hands during our journey and slowly felt excited about the surprise. At the same time hoping it will not be a disappointing activity.

She is confident I will enjoy today and will be the best birthday ever. I have my reservations, as it takes a lot to surprise me.

The driver takes us to the airport, and so I assume we are going somewhere in another state.

Skyla wants today to be our last great day together before we part our ways. 'It is Thursday tomorrow, which is when I have to move out and pick up my key to the new apartment. I will move in the afternoon and starting my new job on Monday. I want you to remember this day, so you never forget me.'

I already have memories I will not forget, 'These past six weeks will stay with me for the rest of my life. I won't forget you. Before I forget, I had a great time.'

Skyla gushes and squeezes my hand. 'I think you love this. Let's get on the plane.'

Before we take off, the pilot speaks over the comms. 'We are about to leave for San Francisco. The flight will be one hour and thirty minutes. The weather is in the high nineteen and is sunny. We will take off promptly. Enjoy the flight.'

Skyla gets annoyed with the part of the surprised being let out of the bag. So, I know where we are going and there is not a lot of interest in me to want to go to SF. But, I will give her the benefit of the doubt.

When we land in San Francisco, Skyla has a taxi to take us to 301 Van Ness Avenue. In the taxi, Skyla is getting excited and is confident I will like my surprise. I assume it will be a restaurant and try to impress me with lavish food. Therefore, I dislike surprises. Friends always cannot pull off a great surprise. They do not listen to what I like. No offense to Skyla, but I have never told her what my interests are.

We arrive at the address and there is a huge gray building with arches along the front with long steps going up to the front. I discrete roll my eyes and promise myself I will not make Skyla feel under appreciative.

I pay the taxi driver, which I think offends her, and walk inside the building.

There are crowds of people in black dresses and black ties. I feel underdressed wearing a casual suit and wonder why she chose a black dress. She could have told me I had to wear a black tie.

Skyla cannot hold her excitement. 'Wait here. I need to get something. I will be right back.'

I politely smile, pretending to be excited, and when she is out of sight, I put on a glum face. A few people walking by politely smile at me and give pleasantry comments. Not sure why they are telling me to enjoy the show. My first thought is it will be a play now and think of 'Juliet and Romeo'. Then it sinks in. She has taken to a play. She does not know I will not like a play. I am going to fall asleep through sheer boredom.

Skyla rushes back. 'Come on. I got it right. I was panicking I screwed up. It shocked me I got a steal on the price. Come on. It will start in about ten minutes. Don't worry about your clothes. I didn't want to the ruin the surprise.'

I fake a smile. 'I will like it because it was you. What is it? "Romeo and Juliet"? "Phantom of the Opera"?'

Skyla scrunches up her face. 'Oh no. I wouldn't subject that to my worst enemy. Think of "Grease" but proper acting.'

I do not see her selling this very well and pretend to get excited. 'Wow. I will pay you a thousand dollars if we are somewhere else.'

Skyla laughs, thinking, I am being funny. 'Come grumpy. No wonder you do not have a girlfriend.'

After several staircases and a long walk in a corridor, we reach a door which opens to a balcony. Despite the play, she found us the best view of the stay and there is an orchestra in front of the stage. I can hear people whispering and the chairs creaking as people take their seats. Once everyone is settled, there is total silence. You can hear a pin drop.

The orchestra is tuning their instruments, and I can hear the violin string and flute being tested. Skyla is still excited and is like a kid waiting for sweets.

The next thing is the curtains pull apart and there is instant music playing, which sounds modern and funky. I wonder what play has present day music.

Skyla is sly and slides to me a brochure. 'Oh. I forgot to give you the programme.'

While staring out across the theater below, I glance at the brochure and see the words 'Hamilton'. I have a second take and then look up at Skyla. Then the play performs.

Skyla has been aware of how down Richard has been throughout the journey. And now, she sees the spark ignite in his eyes and now he is like a child given a toy for his birthday. He becomes fixated, and Skyla feels invisible, but it is a pleasant feeling. She can see all the effort has paid off.

I find myself mesmerized by the play and forget Skyla is next to me. I lean on my elbows over the balcony, consume myself in the play.

After the show finishes, everyone stands up and gives an enormous ovation, including cheers and wolf whistles. I casually clap my hands over Skyla. When the curtain closes and lights come on, I turn to Skyla.

Skyla smiles at me, waiting for my reaction. I go up to her and when she stares at me with a confusing expression, wondering what is up, I kiss her with enthusiasm, which turns into a full, passionate kiss. She smiles, giggles at first when I make a pass at her and then loses herself as we embrace.

We eventually come up for air and I suggest we go back and finish this on the way. But Skyla giggles and has more plans for this evening.

Skyla takes me to a French restaurant on 1454 Grant Avenue at 'Cafe Jacqueline. Skyla pays for the meal as my ongoing birthday surprise. She orders us snails which I have never tried before. Then she orders us frog legs which we both each dare each other to go first. We wash the food down with a bottle of French wine.

She mentions to me how she thinks it knocked her birthday surprise out of the park. I begrudgingly accept her surprise was better and show my gratitude.

After we finish in the restaurant, we go for a stroll for fresh air, walking arm in arm.

I think about our six weeks together. 'It has been nice hanging out with you. Next week will seem boring going back to my old life.'

Skyla feels the same. 'I don't think I am going to enjoy going to a lonely apartment. It will feel weird not seeing you on Monday.'

I do not want it to end. 'Do you have to go tomorrow? We could stay till the end of Sunday.'

Skyla comes up with many reasons. 'I have to move all things into the apartment and sort out my work clothes before I start my new job. I also want time to relax before Monday.'

I feel sad that we only have tomorrow night together. 'Will you need a hand with moving your things?'

Skyla is finding it hard with us going our separate ways, 'I would, but I will find it too hard to say goodbye. You are flying back on Friday and I am sure you have things to do before Monday.'

I wonder if she is around tomorrow night. 'Would you like to come to the party tomorrow? Have one more drink together.'

Skyla does not think it will be a good idea. 'I have too much work to do on Friday and I will need a clear head. I'm not finding excuses.'

I believe her, 'I want to spend time with you.'

Skyla suggests an idea. 'How about we meet up next weekend? Tell you how my new job is going and have a few drinks.'

I would like that, 'Sounds like a plan.'

We continue our walk before heading to the LA.

It is after nine o'clock when we get back and the thought of us not hanging out after tonight puts me in a mood. I am not up to doing anything before bed. Skyla seems deflated herself and does not suggest staying up a little longer.

We both say goodnight and go into our separate rooms.

Skyla toss and turns in her bed, trying to go to sleep. All she can think about is Richard and scared she will never see him again. It has been an entire week of not thinking about Brad. She realizes Brad did her favor to end the relationship, as Richard has taught her what being with someone should be like. Since spending time with Richard, she has had an insight into working as a team and being there for the other person.

She checks the time to see it is only ten o'clock in the evening and gets out of bed and goes to the living room.

When she walks into the living room, it surprised her to see Richard there.

I cannot get to sleep thinking about life being boring when I head back to New York. Skyla has taught me how to have fun and realizing making money is not what makes me happy.

Skyla startles me when I hear her walk in, and we are both wondering why the other is not asleep.

We both find it amusing how we ended up coming into the living room. Skyla comes and sits next to me.

I wonder why she is up. 'Are you overtired?'

Skyla rests her head on the back of the sofa. 'I cannot stop thinking about everything. You?'

I tell her my thoughts, 'I realize life will bore when I head back to New York. I will need to make some changes.'

Skyla realizes the same thing. 'At least you have Nova to hangout with when you get back. I will have no one. All my friends are in relationships.'

I forgot about her. 'I never thought about that. When I return, I will have to call her. I texted her to say thank you for the flowers. She offered to pick me up from the airport. Until she realized I fly privately.'

Skyla finds me amusing. 'Will you end up falling for her?'

I do not know. 'I have only spoken to her once. We haven't even kissed. You have that new guy showing an interest in you.'

Skyla goes quiet. 'Oh, that guy. Yeah, almost forgot about him. Maybe he could be the one.'

I feel kind of jealous she has found someone else. 'Maybe next weekend will get to know him.'

Skyla acts weird. 'I can still find time to hang out with you next weekend. It is not like the hip joins us.'

I realize I want to have one last fling with Skyla before our private lives change forever. 'Can we have more time together?'

Skyla moves her head from the back of the sofa and goes in for a kiss.

While we lock lips, I reach for her breast and caress her while we kiss passionately. I feel her getting aroused instantly as her nipple stiffens. She reaches into my pajama bottoms and strokes the length of my tool. We end up going to the floor with me on top. I watch her unbutton her top until it falls away, leaving her breasts exposed.

I suck on them, hold her nipple between my teeth and gently pull on them. Skyla groans as she enjoys the sensation. I reach down to her vulva and slide two fingers inside. Her hand grasps my wrist to guide my fingers to the right place to get her turned on.

Eventually, she begs me to go inside. I take my top off and pull my bottom off so I am completely naked. Then slide her pajama shorts along her legs and pull them over her feet. I then pull her legs apart.

Skyla admires Richard's chest for the last time while he kneels between her legs. She motions him to place her legs over his shoulders. She waits for him to enter inside her with anticipation. As she feels him slide inside her, there is an instant gasp and wraps her arms around him. She can feel herself getting wet with each thrust. She can feel his balls slapping against her, which adds to the pleasure.

Richard caresses her neck for the first time since they began their intimacy. No one has ever sucked on her neck and, for the first time, finds it an immense turn on. Then he plays with her earlobe, which she finds very sensitive and feels it even more of a turn on.

Skyla wants to change position and lie on her front with Richard entering her from behind. She can feel him rubbing against her vulva and between her cheeks before entering the room. She instantly groans and feels the intensity of her sensitive area being stimulated by him rubbing against it. Her hands guided Richard to grab her breasts and squeeze them as he builds up his rhythm. This is such a turn on for her and wonders why she never done this position before. Eventually she her body stiffens and shudders as waves of ecstasy shoots through her body. When she thinks Richard is going to stop, he raises her hip up in the air and stands on his feet with his knees partially bent. Then continues to pound Skyla and, to her surprise, has more stamina to continue. She really wants Richard to cum inside her and use the muscles in her vulva to tighten round him. Instead, she feels herself having a second wave of orgasm. Richard listens to her body and increases momentum to ensure she cums a second time. He loves watching her body go through the emotions.

Skyla's feet stretches flat out and her legs shake, almost buckling from underneath her. Richard grips her waist so he can continue pounding her until she has no more to give. Eventually she collapses.

I try to control my laughter as I watch Skyla over coming, her multiple orgasm rippling through her body. Skyla pleads me to stop basking in his glory of making her cum so hard. She is disappointed that I did not cum and when she fully recovers, moves herself and rests her back against the sofa. I stand up and move towards her.

Skyla has her eyes fixated on my hard erection. 'I cannot believe you are still hard. Don't sit down. Let me see if I can help relieve you.'

She motions me to stand over her with my legs apart.

Skyla focuses her eyes on his glistening tool coated by her cream. She puts her hand behind his thigh for support as she caresses the end of his manhood with her the tip of her tongue. She can see how much Richard wants to cum as she feels him throbbing. Her attention moves to sliding her tongue along his shaft to clean the mess she left on him.

Richard moves her hair away from her face so he can see her gorgeous facial expression while she works on him. He finds her concentration cute and loves the way she has attention to detail in the way she licks her cream from his length.

Once she finishes, she takes him in her mouth and slowly moves her head back and forth. She rests her arms on the sofa and only her mouth is on him.

I find it an enormous turn on with her arms resting on the sofa while her mouth pleasures me. She moves her head from side to side while continually bobbing her head.

I stand there with my hands by my side, savoring this moment. Skyla glances up at me occasionally to see how close I am to cumming. Skyla is not stopping until I have my orgasm.

Skyla uses her hand to stimulate me and while continuing to work her mouth. I imagine cumming over her face when the time comes. The more I think about, the more I get turned on. Skyla can sense I am about to release my load and speeds up the rhythm. I feel myself about to cum now and make deep breaths and close my eyes to intensify the sensation.

When I feel myself about to burst, I take control and jerk myself. I open my eyes to aim at her breasts. Skyla smiles. Now she knows I am going to cum, and she caresses my thigh in anticipation.

Suddenly, I cum over her breast and Skyla laughs at how much cream has come out and coated her. I give out a load groan as a squeeze to see if there is anymore to squirt out.

Once I have finished releasing myself, there is a little left on the end, and Skyla cleans it away with mouth and makes sure all of it is gone. For another few minutes she continues to give me oral, as she cannot get enough of me.

We eventually go in the shower together to wash ourselves and ensure she has none of me left on her chest. During our shower, we continue to kiss and make our remaining time together count.

She lathers a sponge with plenty of soap and cleans my Johnson, which turns me and makes me erect again. She laughs at how sensitive I am and enjoys seeing me squirm from how sensitive I am.

I return the favor by using a flannel to wash her vulva and reach underneath to cleanse her.

After we have finished, we come out of the shower together and watch each other drying ourselves. We stare at one another in comfortable silence while we appreciate each other's body.

When we are ready for bed, Skyla sleeps in my bed and we spoon each other with my arms around her torso. We gradually drift off to sleep.

Goodbye

Week 6

I naturally wake up panicking that Skyla has already moved out. I feel for her and realize we slept in the same position all night. Skyla is gently stroking my arm with her fingertips. I assume she has been awake for sometime. I rest my chin between her shoulder blades and smell her hair. Skyla realizes I am awake and rolls over to face me.

We stare at each other as we study our faces and realize it is time our last time together.

It is Thursday, and Skyla is moving her things out today. All she has is her clothes and toiletry with her makeup. She is going to have her friend Carla, pick her up and help with her clothes. Then, buy a flat pack bed to put together with her help.

I remember seeing Carla at her company retreat, but I never formerly got introduced and never spoke to her.

Skyla and I are not in a hurry to get out of bed as we lie naked under the bedsheets.

I want to thank for the past six weeks, 'I had a great time with you.'

Skyla has as well, 'You helped me to distract myself from my problems and helped me get my promotion.'

I brush it off. 'You did that by yourself. How are you going to explain about being with another man at work?'

Skyla blushes. 'You know what? I do not know. You will have to come to my future retreats to keep up the pretence. Until I retire.'

I burst out laughing with her. 'I will tell my wife I am away on business. Leave her with the kids.'

Skyla laughs uncontrollably. 'I will tell my husband and kids that no husbands are aloud.'

We continue laughing at the thought.

We finally get out of bed, change, and have breakfast together. Skyla has her last smoothie in the villa, and I have my last coffee and toast.

I wonder when she will leave. 'What time have you arranged for Carla to come over?'

Skyla sips her smoothie. 'Around ten o'clock. Miss the traffic.'

I will be gone by then. 'It will be weird coming back to see you are not here. I don't want to go before you leave.'

Skyla is thinking the same thing. 'But you have your last day in the office.'

After we finish our breakfast, I prepare to leave for work.

Before I leave, we sit on the steps leading up to the front door and properly say our goodbyes. It is hard for both of us to face the reality of our lives going separate ways.

I take out one of my business cards and pass it to her. 'If you are ever in New York, on business or sightseeing, call me. We can go for a coffee. Laugh about what we got up to.'

Skyla nudges me with her shoulder and passes me her business card. 'If you are ever back in town, dealing with your mansion or saving another billion dollar company, look me up. You know where I live.'

I smile and hold her to it. 'I'm glad your friend double booked us. Work would have been depressing.'

Skyla says the same. 'I am glad I got to know you, too.'

I want to tell her something before I regret it. 'If you were not getting over someone and I was living in Los Angeles, I would have asked you on a date. If you said yes, I would have asked if you wanted to go for coffee or see a film.'

Skyla is open-mouthed, 'But what about wanting to be with a black woman and having black children?'

I still want that. 'I would forgo it for you.'

Skyla is speechless. 'Well, I would have said yes. And if you still wanted black babies, I would adopt a pair.'

I laugh and nudge her with my shoulder. 'I don't have any regrets what we got up to.'

Skyla thinks the same. 'Nor do I. I'm glad we did it one more time last night. Any girl will be lucky to have you.'

I have the same thoughts about her, 'Any guy will be proud to have you as their girlfriend.'

We hug each other for a long time before I leave to go to work.

Skyla thinks about her time with Richard before she packs her clothes, makeup, and toiletry.

During her last few weeks with Richard, she has been thinking more about how unhappy she is in her life. Having a glimpse of how she would like to have a relationship and a life makes her reevaluate her life.

While she finishes her packing, she thinks more and more about her future. She has been thinking about what she has regretted not doing. One thing which she always comes back to is traveling.

She originally had plans to move into her apartment today and spend the weekend arranging her things in it. Also, buying a new bed and a few ornaments to make it feel like a home.

The more she pictures herself moving into nVe at 639 N Fairfax, the more depressed she feels. Seeing herself being utterly alone and all she does is go to work. She does not see herself meeting anyone with the life she currently lives.

Skyla has achieved all she wants in her career, and now she wants to find someone and have the relationship she pretended to have with Richard. She cannot do that while she works eighty-hour weeks in a demanding role. It will only get worse in a management role.

After her last night with Richard, it made it even clearer for what she knows she has to do.

Skyla is going to decide to do several things today. First is to ask Carla to take her things to her parents' house instead of the apartment. Second is to go into work today to speak to her boss, Owen, about her decision. Third is to cancel the agreement on the apartment and finally consider where she wants to go.

Carla arrives promptly at ten o'clock to help her friend to carry her things. It does not take Skyla long to pack with what little she has.

Both Skyla and Carla load her things in the car and trunk and leave the villa. Skyla looks behind her and takes one last glance at her home for six weeks.

Carla was interested to know how her six weeks were. 'Did you enjoy your time with Richard?'

Skyla does not go into details. 'It was okay. We got along.'

Carla wonders if they had a fling. 'Did you two get together? He was quite good looking.'

Skyla thinks about last night. 'No. Like I said before, we were just friends, making the best out of an unpleasant situation. He was happy to listen to my problems.'

Carla has a feeling she has fallen for him. 'I think you have a soft spot for him. I saw the way you two looked at each other on the retreat.'

Skyla plays it down. 'That was to give my boss the impression I was married to get that promotion.'

Carla knows something happened between them. 'Have you arranged to meet up again in the future?'

Skyla is vague. 'We swapped business cards, and that's about it. We might meet up. We didn't make definitive plans.'

Carla thinks whatever, 'Even if something happened, you wouldn't tell me, anyway.'

Skyla changes the conversation. 'There is a change of plan. I want to take my clothes to my parents. The apartment is still not ready.'

She gives Carla the address, and it does not take long to reach Skyla's parents' home.

Skyla and Carla unpack the car and take her belongings into the house. Skyla's mum watches them going back and forth between the car and house. Once everything is inside, Skyla anxiously asks her Carla to take her to work. It confused Carla to why she wants to go into work on her day off and the fact they have to buy things for her apartment.

Carla does not question why she is acting strangely today and does as she asks.

When they arrive outside their place of work, Skyla asks her to wait in the car while she goes in.

Skyla feels nervous walking into her boss's office and having the conversation. Owen is curious about why she has come in on her day off.

Owen stays in his chair with a surprise expression. 'What are you doing here?'

Skyla wonders what his reaction will be when she turns down her promotion. 'I have something to say. You will not like it.'

Owen has his interest peeked, 'What is it I will not like?'

Skyla nervously explains, 'I really wanted the promotion. It was my perfect job.'

Owen interrupts, 'Was?'

Skyla takes a breath. 'Let me finish. I got the job on false pretenses. You hinted to get the job. I would have to bring my husband to the retreat. But he is not my husband. I literally have known him for six weeks. I was actually engaged to someone else. But that is another story. The villa was real and how we met.'

Owen's jaw drops. 'You fooled me. It looked real?'

Skyla gives a nervous smile. 'Let me finish. I was desperate for the job, so Richard offered to be my husband.'

Owen has a surprise on his face. 'Maybe you should still have the job. If you can fool two hundred employees, you can do this job. So, don't worry, it is still yours.'

Skyla nervously laughs. 'Everyone keeps thinking we are suited. My family, his family and friends. It was fake. We were lying about being a couple. We don't even want the same thing in a relationship. What I am trying to say is even though I want this job so much, I need to do something I should have got out of my system years ago.'

Owen wonders why the sudden change was, 'Did Richard give you the idea?'

Skyla is abrupt. 'No. But he got me thinking. He really listened to me. He made me find myself again, like when I was twenty-one and sure of my future. I want to go traveling. Get the traveling bug out of my system.'

Owen is still hung up with her relationship. 'And you are going with Richard? Are you sure this was not his idea? I thought you love being around money.'

Skyla scratches her neck from nerves. 'I love my job. But I want to get the traveling bug out of my system. I would like it if I could come back to my old job after I get back.'

Owen has an idea. 'You just want to go traveling. Then come back after seeing the world?'

Skyla never thought of it like that. 'Huh. Yeah.'

Owen smiles. 'Well, why didn't you say? Take sabbatical leave. Your new job will be here when you get back. I will find a temporary manager. It will be like maternity leave. Come back and get into the driver's seat and hit the ground running. How does a year sound?'

Skyla is in shock. 'Are you sure?'

Owen waves her out of the office. 'Go. I will square it with HR. Say hi to Richard for me. He is a great guy.'

Skyla goes to walk out in a daze. 'Thank you. This feels surreal. I thought I was actually giving up my job.'

Owen continues to review some reports. 'Maybe you should get together with Richard. They do not grow on trees. And he is filthy rich.'

Skyla does not know what quite happened and walks out confused, not losing her job. And getting boyfriend advice!'

When she gets back to the car with Carla, she asks her to take her to the apartment so she can get her deposit back. Skyla finally confesses she is canceling the apartment to go traveling. Explaining the reason she came into work on her day off.

After Skyla gets back to her parents' house from canceling the apartment, she separates her clothes for traveling. She gathers her thoughts of what to pack and leave behind.

Company Ball

♥

It is slowly becoming a reality for Skyla. She will leave the country, which scares her in a good way. On the way back from the apartment, she found a flight for tomorrow to fly to Tahiti. When she is almost finishing her packing, Richard pops into her head and she reminisces about her time with him.As she thinks about the baseball game, she laughs to herself and the time at her retreat. Then she thinks about the times they kissed and made love. As she remembers those times, she realizes she has formed feelings for Richard and never realized.She told herself it was a friend with benefits or a FB relationship. But not being with him now has made her realize how much she misses him and wishes she was still with him. But, she keeps remembering that he wants a black woman and unless there is a miracle or she goes under the sun bed and bakes herself to death, he won't be interested.Her mum comes into her bedroom. 'Are you finished packing?'

Skyla procrastinates with clothes in her hands. 'Mum, there is something I need to tell you.'

Her mum is dubious. 'What is that?'

Skyla tells her the truth. 'Brad was not Brad.'

Her mum giggles quietly. 'I already know. Your sister looked at your social media account. Even though you don't use it, you linked Brad to your relationship. They tried to learn more about him by looking at his social media account that day. At the family's birthday party. And behold, it was a white man.'

Skyla laughs, which then sets them both off. 'What was I thinking? I should have just told you the truth. Brad dumped me six weeks ago, and I felt like a failure and embarrassed. I thought my brother and sisters would look at me with pity. They are all married and with kids. All I have is a job and don't even own a house.'

Her mum holds Skyla in her arms. 'Don't you ever dare think that. I am so proud of you. You are going to go traveling and see the world. How many people are brave enough to give up their job just like that?'

Skyla wells up. 'Well, I am on sabbatical leave. Do you think I will find someone?'

Her mum wells up. 'Yes, you will. He will be funny, gel with the family instantly and dote on you. He will make you happy. Just like how Richard did. I never saw you so happy that day. I swear you were together by the way you two almost made out in front of the children that day when playing baseball. You two were so embarrassed when the kids caught you going to kiss or make out.'

Skyla does not remember. 'Oh please. It was nothing like that. We had got caught up in the moment of winning.'

Her mum cuts her eyes. 'Every time I mention his name, your eyes light up. You look away as if you are recalling a moment.'

Skyla still brushes it off by laughing. 'It is only because I have a laugh with him.'

Her mum is unconvinced. 'Maybe it was meant to be you and Brad ending. Maybe it was meant to be your friend double booking the villa. Maybe it was meant to be for you and Richard to be stuck together for six weeks.'

Skyla does not know. 'We have different wants. He wants a black woman. I want someone who will make me laugh and make me be myself.'

Her mum ticks her off, 'Go to him. Tell him your true feelings. Throw your chips in the air and let them lay where they fall. If he says no, then go traveling.'

Skyla is confident there are no feelings there. 'He sees me as a friend. Nothing more.'

Her mum tests her, 'What is the best time you have ever had?'

Skyla thinks hard. 'Going to Mexico. And my company retreat. Why?'

Her mum smiles, 'Who was that with?'

Skyla goes quiet, 'Richard.'

Her mum makes her come to her senses. 'You didn't even have to think about it.'

Skyla now has regrets. 'Right. I will see him. Tell him how much I think I like him. Only to shut you up.'

The ball is getting lively, and I sit at a table by myself and ponder on my time with Skyla. Also, mentally planning my day tomorrow by catching the plane back with my people.

I have had a lot of thought over the past six weeks and I am going to take a year off work and focus on my well being. Simon can manage the firm while I am away. Not sure what I will do to find happiness.

John comes up to my table and asks to sit with me. 'I can't believe where we are. You found the employee who was trying to sabotage my company. Drag us into the 21 century and here you sit as if it is all in a day's work. Thank you, Richard.'

I raise my shot glass with my one of my favorite spirits, 'No problem. What will you do now?'

John is not sure as he thinks about it. 'I think I will pass the reins over to my grandson. And step back.'

I cheer him on that. 'He will do a great job. I am having Mark stick around to help. I think he is ready.'

John asks about my future. 'Are you going to take time off work?'

I tell him my thoughts. 'I have been thinking about it. Looking at possibly hanging around here for a while. See what LA offers. Then probably go traveling abroad.'

John wonders about Skyla. 'Have you told her how much you love her?'

I almost choke on my drink. 'What?'

John has a dead-pan face. 'Have you told her how much you love her?'

I laugh off what I see is nonsense. 'We are friends. She is still in love with Brad. And I am ready to find the love of my life. Love. How do you know when you are in love?'

John gives me an example, 'When you wake up tomorrow and she is not there. If you find yourself sniffing her pillow and going into each room to find her. Your heart misses her after only six hours, then ask yourself if you love her.'

I brush off his theory. 'I won't be doing that. I have a lot on tomorrow. As soon as I wake up, I have to pack and give back the keys. Meet up with my team and fly back to New York. Then sort out my affairs before coming back here or getting on a plane to another country.'

John half laughs, 'Well, think of me when you wake up tomorrow. You feel a dull pain here in your heart. Like she died and you are grieving for her loss. You suddenly have this deep regret of not telling her how you really feel. Trust me.'

I still do not believe him. 'That is the older generation. This generation is internet dating swiping the screen left. I don't miss her now. I won't miss her tomorrow. One thing for sure is I won't miss how untidy she is. And the way she twirls her hair when she is procrastinating. The way she uses me as an armchair. The way she... stares at me when our eyes lock.'

John thinks I am trying to fool myself. 'We will wait and see. Give me a call if I am wrong. And tell me I am wrong. If I don't hear from you, I know you are going to see about a girl.'

With that, he gets up and leaves me to myself. I briefly laugh to myself at the prospect of pining for Skyla. I really like her as a friend but not enough to have missed her and wish she was still here. Besides, she is not going anywhere. She will be at work tomorrow and settling into her new apartment over the weekend. Knowing where she will be will not make me miss her over night.

As I stare into my glass, I sense someone is standing in front of the table. For a second I think it is another invited guest to the party.

I am shocked to see it is Nova.

No One Compares To You

♥

I think I have had too much to drink and mistaking her for someone else.

Nova is not sure whether to smile or worry. 'Surprise.'

I wonder what she is doing here. 'How did you find me?'

Nova reminds me of the text, 'You gave the address where you are.'

I remember now, 'But, I thought it was a matter-of-fact question. To make conversation,'

Nova feels unwanted, 'Not pleased to see me?'

I quickly make her feel welcome. 'Oh, of course. Take a seat.'

She is very attractive in a flowing black dress with a sheen and everyone in the room is staring at her. I feel like I should be the lucky guy to have her sat next to me.

Not sure how to behave around her. She has caught me off my guard.

I want to know what is happening here, 'Did you come here to have fun or to find a relationship?'

Nova says nothing and lingers in for a kiss with her eyes closed. My first reaction is to move away, and Nova opens her eyes to see my reaction. As she pulls away, I feel guilty and my knee jerk reaction is to kiss her to make her feel less uncomfortable.

Skyla arrived five minutes earlier, trying to find Richard. By the time she spots him, Richard is kissing Nova like how he kisses her. It throws Skyla, and she hides behind a pillar next to the table. She catches her breath and her heart sinks to see he is with Nova. She assumes he invited her to the ball for a plus one guest. And now she sees them together.

She begins to well up after seeing them kiss passionately and runs off before they notice her here. She is relieved not to have embarrassed herself in front of them.

When we pull away, I regret making a pass at her. Even though she was a good kisser, it did not feel natural, and she does not compare to Skyla. I do not know if I have been round Skyla too long or not kissed enough women. But Nova did not give me the same buzz as Skyla did.

Skyla hails a taxi and, while traveling in the back, she leans her head against the window and stares out into the black night. Tears are streaming down her face as she faces yet another rejection.

She has a thought and asks the taxi driver to take her to Carlyle Avenue, North Montana.

Carla is finishing deserts with her husband and two kids in the dining room. She hears the doorbell, not expecting anyone tonight. She checks the time and sees it is after ten o'clock and wonders who would be calling at this time now.

She moans at her husband while she goes to the front door, expecting it to be one of his friends.

When she opens the door, she sees it is her friend in floods of tears and waiting for a hug from her best friend. Carla quickly sweeps her into her arms like she would with one of her children before she falls down.

Skyla wails in tears. 'He doesn't like me. I think I am in love with him and he doesn't want me.'

Carla squeezes her in her arms. 'It's okay. I'm here. There, there.'

Half an hour later, Skyla calms down and the two are sitting in the kitchen drinking coffee together. Carla waits patiently for her to open up.

Skyla glares at her half-empty mug of coffee. 'Got anything stronger?'

Carla smiles. 'We don't drink. What happened?'

Skyla recounts what she saw. 'After speaking to my mum, I drivel myself into thinking that I am falling for him. I go the ball where his client has a celebration party, saving the company from going bust. Well, stupidly think to surprise him and show my feelings. But, when I find him, He is kissing Nova passionately. Like how kisses me.'

Carla has missed sixty seconds. 'Woah, back up. Who is Nova? And you told me nothing happened between you two.'

Skyla realizes she has confessed to a fling. 'Nova is someone his brother introduced to at a family get together last weekend. He must have invited her not long after he left for work. And to think I slept with him last night.'

Carla's eyes nearly pop out, 'What! You slept with him too? I can't believe you lied to me.'

Skyla is still thinking about last night. 'I am the one hurting here.'

Carla tries to show empathy while wondering how they got together. 'Of course. Carry on. The bit about how you got together last night.'

Skyla scours at her. 'Okay, we've been sleeping with each other since the retreat. Before that, we occasionally kissed. It felt natural to sleep together that night. Then, we did it last night. If I had known he had plans to be with her, I would have never gone tonight.'

Carla feels sad for her friend. 'Maybe it's a good time you go traveling?'

Skyla continues to be tearful. 'I thought I left the emotion out of it. Just two good friends choosing to have a fling with no attachment. I did not know I would end up falling for him. We were only co-habitan for six weeks. What idiot creates feelings for someone else while getting over an ex fiance. Who does that?'

Carla calms her down. 'Well, you are here now. It is not how you got here. What are you going to now?'

Skyla has already concluded. 'I leave tomorrow. I use the time to get over two people. There is nothing I can do. He already told me he wants to marry and have kids with a black woman. Keep it inside his culture. And now he has. Oh Carla, she is like a model. Even if I had a shot, why would he choose me over her?'

Carla reaches out for her hand. 'Well, his loss. You have a lot going for you. Any man will love to have you. You will meet him on your travels.'

Skyla laughs through her tears. 'He was great in bed. I liked how his...'

Carla closes her ears. 'la la la la la. I don't want to know about your sex life. I am married and stuck with the same guy. I don't want to picture you two doing it.'

After Skyla comes over her emotions and Carla gives her advice of using the trip to heal old wounds, she finally leaves and goes back to her parents.

The next day, Skyla wakes up early and spends the morning having breakfast with her parents. It is an emotional day as their last child will fly the coup to hopefully one day come home with a husband.

Go After Her

♥

Skyla has her bags packed and gets ready to head to the airport. She knows she has to be there two hours before the flight. There is plenty of time, as her flight is not until five o'clock this afternoon. They don't have to leave until half-past two to get there at three o'clock.

After breakfast, only Skyla and mum are still sitting at the breakfast table.

Her mum is tearful. 'I cannot believe you going to do this. I cannot believe your company is encouraging you to take sabbatical leave to do this.'

Skyla wells up. 'Please, keep it together. You are setting me off.'

Her dad gives her a hug. 'Be careful. Make you have enough mosquito repellent. Don't go off with any strangers. And find me a son-in-law. You are my last child to settle down.'

Her mum asks about her friend. 'Have you said goodbye to Richard already?'

Skyla huffs at her, 'We said our goodbyes yesterday. And besides, he is not into me.'

Her mum can see the sadness in her eyes. 'Oh. You really love him. I can see it in your eyes. Why don't you go after him?'

Skyla thinks about the conversation she overheard. 'Oh mum, why doesn't anyone want me? I have a... had a great job. Still do. Have no baggage.'

Her mum chokes as she clutches her neck, 'Oh baby. You will meet someone. They will love all of you.'

Her dad really liked her pretend boyfriend. 'Why don't you go back to Richard and ask him to choose between her and you? Before you head to Tahiti? Just tell him how much you like him. If he says no, then leave.'

Skyla knows it is too late, as he has flown back to New York. 'He has gone back home. He has a million dollar company to run. Why would he put work aside to see if we would make it?'

Her dad is curious to how they departed, 'Did he give you his number? Did you agree to see each other again?'

Skyla remembers the business card. 'Yeah. He said to call him if I had nothing to do. But that was before he hooked up with Nova.'

Her dad feels like she is cutting off the conversation. He says nothing more.

I naturally wake up and check what time it is to see that it is only seven o'clock. I feel like I am on vacation with no work to sort out and no office meeting to go to. For a second, I was looking forward to seeing Skyla next door, but immediately remember she moved out to her new apartment.

I wanted to tell Skyla what happened last night and tell her how I realized Nova was not my type.

Nova wanted to stay at the villa but I made it cleared there would not be an opportunity to see where the relationship goes. My gut feel told me she was not the one. The moment I realized, was soon after we kissed, when Skyla came into my head. It was her I wish was kissing.

When I get out of bed and wonder around the villa aim-
lessly, I can visualize her in each room. I remember our first
encounter, startling her by the swimming pool.

I can still smell her from each room and I go into her
bedroom and going up to her pillow and breathing her in. I
soon snap out of it and feel like I am mourning her death.
We were only friends and wondered why I was behaving like
this. I know she is not the one for me, even though she was a
natural kisser and knew how to press my button. Yes, we slept
together, but we were both drunk and both quickly regretted
it. So, why do I pine for her company?

I get in the shower to distract myself from thinking too
much about her and trying to find her scent to hold on to her.
But the shower is not taking my mind off. I feel my stomach
turning into knots at the thought of never seeing her again.

I frantically dry myself and changing into my suit and
preparing to stop over to her place of work, just to see her
one more time. Before I head off to the airport to catch my
flight with my colleagues.

Once I am dressed, I check the time, and it is gone by eight
o'clock. I decide to call the limousine to come pick me up.

I arrive at her place of work really nervous and walk inside
the lobby to reception. I see a lady behind the desk asks if she
can help me, and I ask for Skyla. While I wait for her to contact
her office, I wait nervously wondering what I am going to say
to her.

The lady asks my name and tells the person on the phone
who I am. There is a pause and told someone is coming down
to see me.

I take a seat and stare at the floor, rehearsing my lines about
what I am going to tell her. After five minutes, I wonder if they

forgot about me until a woman's pair of feet appears in front of me. I glance up, assuming it is Skyla, and a woman with short brunette hair stares at me.

The woman is curious to ask, 'Are you Richard Lewis?'

I gesture to her, 'Yes. Is Skyla busy to see me?'

The woman smiles at me. 'I am a friend of Skyla. My name is Carla. You must be the guy who was living with her.'

I do not know how she would know, as I have never heard of her. 'Huh. That is right. I guess she told you about me.'

Carla cannot stop smiling. 'Have you come to give her something or ask her something?'

I am not sure what she means. 'There is something I need to say to her. It is personal. Can you tell her it is important that I need to see her and I can wait for her? Get a coffee and wait.'

Carla changes from being happy to showing a long face. 'Skyla has left the company. She quit on Thursday. She has taken sabbatical leave and is heading to Tahiti.'

My heart sinks. 'When is she leaving? Do you know what airport?'

Carla does not know what airport she is flying from. 'Sorry. Was it important?'

I get desperate, 'Can I get her parents' address? Wait, I have an idea.'

I think of the apartment she was meant to move into. When someone finally picks, they tell me she canceled the lease agreement. I then remembered something and phone my office to get hold of her mum taxes file. My hand twitches while I wait for someone to pickup. Eventually, someone answers.

I speak a million miles. 'It is Richard. There is a tax file on a Janice Parker. I need her address. I need it fast.'

After a couple of minutes, my employee finds her details on the computer and I ask her to take a picture and text it to me.

I turn to Carla. 'Thank you for your help. I have to go and see about a girl.'

Carla has something to say. 'Ever since she met you, her face would always glow when I mentioned your name. You take care of my friend. Make her happy.'

I smile at her, 'I promise. Nice meeting you. If things work out, I will see you again.'

Carla quietly laughs. 'Go get her.'

I run out of the building and into the limousine. I show him my cell phone and tell him to drive me there.

When I arrive outside her parents' home in a quiet suburb, I run to the front door. After I ring the doorbell, I compose myself and check that I am presentable. The door opens, and it is her dad.

I wonder if he remembers me, 'Hi. I am a friend of your daughter. Skyla. Can I come in briefly?'

Her dad allows me in, 'Your the fake boyfriend. Richard. I will get her mother.'

I guess he must have seen my business card. 'Thanks. One thing. Would you mind if I date your daughter? Not that you would, considering you thought we were dating.'

Her dad shakes his head and walks away. I hear him shout out his wife's name.

Janice finally walks in and wonders why I am here. 'What can I do for you?'

I feel nervous expressing my feelings. 'I heard Skyla quit her job. She is going traveling. I wanted to know if she had left already. I rang reception at the apartment she was meant to move into. She is not there. You are the only person I could think of who might know.'

Janice is curious about why I want to find and makes an assumption. 'Skyla told me you were not into her. Do you like my daughter?'

I do not feel comfortable telling her my feelings, 'I just need to tell something. Before it is too late.'

Janice already knows when she stares into my eyes, 'She is leaving from LAX. Her flight is at 13.15. You leave now, you might just catch her.'

I think worst-case scenario, 'Do you have an address in Tahiti? Worst case I fly out there.'

Janice is opened mouthed, 'You do know she is going traveling.'

I smile at her, 'I just quit my job, that I own. I am going to spend my time trying to convince Skyla to have me.'

Janice grins at me. 'Welcome to the family. Does this mean I will get free financial advice for life?'

I laugh, 'Absolutely.'

With that, I run out of the house and head to the airport. I have to do is search for the flight time to Tahiti on the screen. Then find the terminal she will be boarding from.

While traveling to the airport, I get my cell phone out and call my coworkers that I will not make the flight.

Caroline, Jessica, Simon and Alina are already at 'Los Angeles Private Jet Charter - Travel King International', waiting to fly back to New York. They have been here only a few minutes and are already on the plane waiting for their boss. Simon gets a call and sees it is Richard.

Simon answers the phone. 'Yep. Where are you?'

I hear him on the phone. 'I am going to be running late. There is a... something I need to do. It is something important to sort out.'

Simon thinks it is the client. 'There is no other problem, is there?'

I quickly reassure him, 'No. It is nothing to do with Jim. Everything is okay now. Mark is taking the helm. There is something personal I have to do.'

Simon guesses what it is. 'It is not that girl, right?'

I go quiet and feel embarrassed. 'What if it is?'

Simon sounds like he is laughing. 'We will see you later. I think you will be awhile. Don't come back until you get her.'

I guess I am actually going to get a girlfriend, 'I will see you guys later. Take care of the firm.'

Simon seems to know that I have feelings for her. 'I had a funny feeling you would eventually be ready to take time off work and focus on your private life. You deserve it. I will make sure the firm ticks over while you are away. Goodbye Lewis.'

I cannot believe this is me turning my back on work and, for the first time, putting me first, 'I don't even know if she likes me.'

When I reach the airport, I run into departure and find a screen to find her flight. I panic when I cannot find her flight. Scratching my head, I go to find a customer desk.

The person behind the desk looks up the flight for me and tells me that the plane will be boarding soon. Once I find which terminal number it is, I sprint there.

It takes me ten minutes to reach the departure lounge. I scour the area looking for a blonde hair and guess what should would be wearing.

Skyla goes to pick up her luggage and is startled when she notices me as she straightens up. 'What are you doing here?'

I see her stunned to see me. 'Can we go somewhere in private? If you miss the plane, you can use my private jet. It will take you anywhere you want to go. Please.'

Skyla is conscious of everyone in the lounge staring at us. 'I am about to board. How did you find me? I never told you I was going traveling.'

I put my hands out to ask her to wait and hear me out. 'I know. But, if I don't say this, I will regret it for the rest of my life. I will walk into my office back to my normal life. Alone again. Utterly alone. Wishing that I said this.'

Skyla glances over at the boarding stand, not knowing how to react. 'I find that hard to believe. Last night, I saw you with Nova. I saw you two kissing. Why aren't you with her now?'

Everyone in the lounge notice the commotion and stops what they are doing to listen in.

I gather my thoughts and am willing to have this conversation with people around us. 'Okay. Okay. I was not expecting that. She kissed me first. Then, to make her feel less embarrassed, I kissed her back. Then, I eventually pulled away.'

Skyla scoffs. 'You don't have to rub it in. I get it. She is black. She is who is what you want to be with. She is a model. Makes me feel below average.'

I smile at how cute she is when she is jealous. 'Shut up. Shut up. When I kissed her, I realized she wasn't you. She wasn't in the same vicinity as you. Not even close. Before I met you, I already had plans to slow down and figure out a way of trying to meet someone. Worried and scared that even if I spent my life solely finding someone, it still wouldn't happen. Then I met you. Without realizing it, I actually got the experience of being in a relationship. A marriage, but without the kids. And you know what? I loved it. I loved meeting your family and feeling a part of them. I felt I belonged with them. I loved going to Mexico with you. That will be the closest thing to a honeymoon. I loved the way you kissed me. The way you scratch your neck when you get nervous, like you are doing right now. I love the way you wear your hair. I love it when I make you laugh. And I love you. There I said it. I love you. It has only been six weeks. But it felt like six months. And I know you don't feel the same way, but I had to tell you how I felt so I could get closure. I never live with regret. I don't want to start now. I know you are still getting over your ex-boyfriend and your heart does not have enough room to love anyone else. Even if you did like me. I read it can take eleven weeks minimum to get over someone. So, that's it. Have a safe trip. After you finish traveling and for some reason, you still have not met someone, which I highly doubt it. Maybe you would want to go for a coffee...'

Skyla wells up, almost crying, and not sure if I have offended her or making her miss her flight, 'Stop. Stop. Stop. Talk about bad timing.'

I just want to say one more thing. 'The hardest part was finding you and realizing that you are the one for me. The easy part was falling in love with you. How I wish you would love me. I will settle for liking me.'

Skyla drops her bag from her shoulder and saunters over to me. I wonder if she is going to hit me or shout at me for embarrassing her.

I quickly apologize, 'Sorry for...'

Before I can finish my sentence, she pounces on me and kisses me fully on the lips. She continues to press her lips against mine and I eventually reciprocate.

During our kiss, I gradually hear the other passengers cheering and clapping, including the boarding woman. We eventually pull away, feeling embarrassed.

I try to apologize again, 'Sorry to embarrass you.'

Skyla rubs her nose against mine and smiles. 'Your city or mine?'

I smile right back and kiss her. 'I have that mansion in Beverly Hills.'

Skyla laughs. 'You made me find myself again.'

I correct her, 'No. You made me find myself again.'

A year later, her family had another family get together at the same park and I they once again welcomed me. This time I was her fiance, and it was our engagement party.

Thank you so much for buying and reading my book!!

Can you please leave a STAR RATING? NO WRITTEN REVIEW REQUIRED

US:

http://www.amazon.com/review/create-review?&asin=B0041JKFJW

UK:

https://www.amazon.co.uk/review/create-review?&asin=B004H4XAXO

DE: https://www.amazon.de/review/create-review?&asin=0765365278

Subscribe for new future e-book releases below.

Jane Knight Rogue Officer
  Blind Love
  Eternity Wing And A Pray
  Jane Knight Fair Game
  To The Stars
  Ponta Delgada A Good Place To Die
  Jane Knight A Spy Among Us
  Jane Knight Tomorrows World
  By Chance
  Cold Bones
  All e-books are available at leonmaedwards.com to see all good online retail stores.

BOOKS ALSO BY LEON M A EDWARDS
Jane Knight Rogue Officer
Blind Love
Eternity Wing And A Pray
Jane Knight Fair Game
To The Stars

Ponta Delgada A Good Place To Die
Jane Knight A Spy Among Us
Jane Knight Tomorrows World
All e-books are available at leonmaedwards.com to see all good online retail stores.

The link above will take you to my subscription page

Join Leon M A Edwards mailing list for a free e-book and future new releases.

GET A FREE E-BOOK NOW!

Printed in Great Britain
by Amazon